N. Haq grew up in India and travelled extensively within India.

She completed her graduation in medicine, and came to England for further studies, in the late 90s.

Her personal life has been difficult, and being so far away from her country and her family makes everything more challenging.

N. Haq strives with strife and this story depicts her fight for survival and independence.

This book is dedicated to my parents, the two most beautiful and most forgiving people in the world.

To my dear brother for putting up with me, and my long-suffering hubby for his patience.

N. Haq

THE STORY OF MOLLY MITTER

AUSTIN MACAULEY PUBLISHERS™

LONDON • CAMBRIDGE • NEW YORK • SHARJAH

A CIP catalogue record for this title is available from the British Library.

ISBN 9781035828067 (Paperback)
ISBN 9781035828074 (ePub e-book)

www.austinmacauley.co.uk

First Published 2024
Austin Macauley Publishers Ltd®
1 Canada Square
Canary Wharf
London
E14 5AA

I would like to thank the team at Austin Macauley Publishers for their support and consideration throughout the process.

I would also like to thank my family and close friends for their support.

My special gratitude to Sanjeeta Ahmed for the cover.

Chapter 1

Molly sat at her desk, waiting. It had been a long day and she could not think any more. There were so many things going on inside her head that she almost heard whirring wheels and cogs inside.

She had left Molloy four years back, walked out of her only home in a foreign land and now she lived alone in a flat.

This was a new Molly, she thought—someone who will not take things lying down, someone who will put her foot down and protest in a grown-up fashion.

No more crying, screaming and slashing her skin, not anymore. That is no way to protest. She clearly remembered picking up a shard of broken glass from the floor and cutting her arm from her wrist to her elbow. She would also go into the toilet with a knife and cut her legs, her arms, anywhere really.

She had read somewhere that cutting did not hurt, and that when you saw the blood, that somehow relieved the pain. She had tried telling a friend over the phone but her friend sounded shocked and dismayed that Molly could say such a thing. She did not understand.

To everyone, Molly was a bubbly happy woman always ready for a laugh. Her three lovely kids, her beautiful house, her witty husband had all helped strengthen that image.

Very few people guessed that underneath this glossy exterior was a deeply unhappy woman who did not have any love in her life. Little did they guess that the smiling witty Molloy was a cold-hearted man flirting with other women, who already had several 'lady friends'.

Molly knew that women liked Molloy for the same reasons that she had liked him as a fresher in first year of college but now she felt insecure and unhappy, especially when she saw how much he craved feminine attention, fully knowing how much it hurt Molly; it was almost perverse. Molly loved him with all her heart and wanted to be loved back, wanted to do all the things that other couples did. Molloy never took her picture, never took her out and bought the same jewellery set for their anniversary every year. She wished he would be more spontaneous.

As a young girl, Molly was simple, quiet and hardworking—the sort of daughter every parent wants and the sort of student every teacher desires.

Molly's mum would go to her parents evening each year and come back, not saying a word about the meeting at home. Others might have been worried but Molly knew why because the feedback was all good, Mum did not have anything to 'report'.

Then came the day when she had to choose a career path and her parents wanted her to be a doctor, no surprises there. Molly wanted to be an investigative journalist, the sort that goes into war zones and other dangerous areas, rescues the elderly and infirm and takes prize-winning photos.

Molly felt that would be her right calling. She hated any routine, any schedule; she hated convention; investigative journalism had the right mix of adventure and philanthropy. Yes, that was perfect for Molly as an awesome career.

However, when she spoke to her parents she could see that they did not share her enthusiasm for journalism, they thought it was very unsafe for a young woman in India. Molly knew she wanted her parents to be proud of her so she chose medicine over journalism and the very day she was due to sit the journalism entrance, she took the train to medical school. Fait accompli indeed.

Med school was a whole new chapter.

The gruelling entrance exams, the fine art of survival in a girl's hostel, travelling alone on local trains, studying 10–12 hrs. A day for her semesters and doing everything, repeating everything on a shoestring. Before medical school, railway stations were a novelty; they smelt of holidays in faraway lands. Molly always travelled in first class with family, the deep seats, the soft blankets, the trays of warm food covered in crisp white cloth napkins.

Here she was lucky to get a seat on the train, the trains smelt of cheap cigarettes and sweat and old poo and the people were vicious. They wanted to touch her on any pretext.

Molly felt that she was somehow guilty of being born to a decent middleclass family and that people eyed her with mistrust and deep disdain. The moment you sat next to a woman, she asked you probing questions nonstop until she had your life history in graphic detail. If it was a man, they tried to come closer and closer and pretended to fall asleep so they could touch her body as if unknowingly. Molly became used to shouting and protesting against these men and even when she was married, her husband was always busy minding something else, say the luggage or something and Molly had to fend for herself. She never felt safe or protected and railway stations had now become scary places.

When she first fell in love with Molloy, she did crazy things because that was the kind of person she was. She wrote and told her dad about her feelings, something none of her friends ever did. But Molly lived by her own rules, she believed honesty was the best policy.

Her parents were shocked but did not show it hoping this was a crush and would soon blow over.

Did they not know Molly at all?

Right after they got together, Molly pleaded with Molloy to move to a bigger hospital to further his career. Molloy was not sure but agreed after a lot of coaxing.

They were now separated by a few hundred miles of poor transport and very shaky phone lines; mobile phones did not exist then.

Molly used to ring Molloy once a fortnight, usually a Saturday because making a phone call was expensive. She had to take a rickshaw to the town centre, find a phone booth and make the call from there. The phone charges halved after seven in the evening, off peak as we call it now. So, Molly would go early and wait in line for the after-seven calls. She thought nothing of it then. It was normal.

Once there was a state-wide power failure and she heard that the nearest place where she could make a call was four hours. On the local bus. So, Molly got on the crowded local bus and travelled for four hours. Just to speak to Molloy on the phone.

One time Molloy had gone to Delhi for his postgrad entrance and Molly knew on his way back, his train would pass through a station three hours. From her hostel.

As soon as Molly found out, she enlisted the help of one of her seniors in college to help her go and see Molloy. Her classmates did her hair and helped her get ready for the meeting, they could see her excitement and happiness.

Molly took the bus to the train station, met the station master and told him a terrible cock and bull story just to get Molloy's name announced at the station when the train stopped for five minutes. The announcement was that there was an emergency and he needed to come off the train straightaway.

A completely crazy idea and Molly was not sure it would work. Molloy might be asleep; he would miss the announcement then. The plan actually worked perfectly but Molly wished it hadn't.

Once he got off the train, Molloy was very angry.

He did not like his journey disrupted, he wanted to get back on the train straightaway. The train stopped for only a few minutes but there was another one in an hour that he could take. The senior who had escorted Molly tried to calm him down but he was not having any of it. He wanted to get back on the train.

The loud knocking on the door awoke her from her reverie. "Hi Doctor, are you all right?"

"I am fine, Sara, can you send the next patient in please?"

Chapter 2

Dear Anita,

It was so good to bump into you.

Mona had mentioned the other week that you were in town, given me your number and I had promised that I would call you as soon as I got home but you know what happens as soon I reach home; there's roughly a million things needing my immediate attention and my own needs are at the very bottom—no more complaints, promise.

Are you chuffed to get a letter from me, you must be. I remember writing to you from medical school and what a great time we had writing to each other. You telling me all about your stylish English literature life compared to my own blood, sweat and tears life in medicine.

How's everyone at home? Are you married? Do you have kids? I miss going over to your house after school. Remember the big open terrace with your grandma's pickles drying in the sun and your mum's favourite gardenias at the other end. I was far more interested in the pickles then but now I might wander over to the flowers and smell their summery fragrance.

Remember we were too busy sitting on a jute mat on the terrace eating muri with spicy potato cutlets and green chillies to think of flowers. I remember your servant used to water them every evening just after sunset, when the heat died down and cool breeze blew from the east.

I remember waking up to the sound of bells and chanting at least once a month and I and Sam, my little brother, would go running over to your house for Narayan puja.

By the time we jumped out of bed, washed and ran over, the puja would be well underway with the priest chanting and offering flowers and lamps while the others beat the small clanger, the kanshor and the big one called the ghanta which was really a large metal plate that you sounded with a wooden hammer.

I remember my brother, being younger, would take the kanshor and I with all the grace and composure of a sister who was a full eighteen months older, not a day less, would proudly take the ghanta. I remember your mum would be busy laying out the fruit and sweets offerings and you were always next to her, helping.

It was not easy beating the ghanta, because with your left hand, you had to swing the heavy metal plate and with your right hand, you had to bring down the wooden hammer to hit it at a regular pace but if anyone ever said—is this too heavy for you—I would never ever admit that it was too heavy for me; it was always—no no I am fine thanks. Better die than admit it was too heavy for me.

After the puja was over, I remember sitting down in a long line on the floor with banana leaves in front of us, the water was served in conical glasses made of terracotta, called khuree.

It felt so good all of us sitting and eating together. I remember you and Sam hated pineapples so all the pineapple pieces came to me, I was not a fan of coconut and neither were you so all the coconut chunks went to Sam, we all knew what the others did or did not like. It was so comfortable.

I wonder if you still live there, you lucky girl.

I still remember it was a large old house with shiny red cement floors with very high ceilings and high staircases. Do you remember one of the rooms had a half door, like you see in old westerns or in some old barber shops in Kolkata, I always wondered who put that in the middle of the house but never asked.

You had a really big old fridge, was it German? Electrolux, I think. It was one of the first in the neighbourhood so that if anyone needed ice (usually a child after a bump on the head), you were the first port of call, just like if anyone needed the phone, they came to ours; it was normal and no one thought anything of it back then.

The rooms were built around a central courtyard same as our house and each room had many doors and many windows. I remember the massive fish tank and the cage of budgies that your older brother used to look after. The budgies were really friendly though I remember not being very keen on them.

I was a quiet bookish person and I still remember an astrology prediction about my pets—"self-caring dog or cat that will stay outside"—sums it up nicely I thought then.

As kids we were not allowed in the garden which of course meant that it was on the top of our list of places we must visit.

It is strange how I remember the exact site of the old wooden door connecting the house and the garden. The door was smooth and heavy and although it had sagged a little with time, it opened easily enough when you turned the rusty old knocker on the side.

Entering the garden was like stepping into another world, the moist earth smelt heavenly and large trees leafy trees dappled the light beautifully. The ground felt soft and wet to our naked feet and the smell of the earth was intoxicating.

We could see the emerald green pond at the end of the garden shining brightly in the sun, as if the garden had ended suddenly, like a poem stopping in the middle of a sentence.

I remember the pond surrounded by a high wall made of old bricks and covered with greenish yellow moss that glistened in the sun. The sunlight over the pond and surrounding walls crisscrossed and made tiny prisms of light on the water, fleeting prisms that would remind Molly of a hit song now but back then she had not heard of Pink Floyd.

Maybe the secret garden and the pond have now been replaced by a concrete apartment block with underground parking, progress I say, but please let's not go there.

Do you remember the house next to ours?

The lady of the house was a famous singer and was busy practising and teaching students all day. The only other time we saw her was when she took her son to the school bus.

We all waited for it on weekday mornings. The school bus sounded its horn at 7:30 am sharp and you would hear a commotion arising from their house and if you peeped out, you would see that this was coming from a small procession moving from their house towards the school bus. Bhutun the little boy was always at the forefront screaming and crying and saying he did not want to go to school the second place was his mum, who was trying to brush his hair, put his shirt and tie on and calm him, all at the same time.

The third place was taken by the ayah who would be carrying the water bottle, lunchbox, schoolbag and his shoes and socks. His dad we knew was a geologist and worked somewhere far away with wild tribal people and malarial mosquitoes, so we hardly ever saw him. Something tells me now that he rather preferred the poisoned arrows and the malaria to this. The bus standing there honking, all the little boys looking out and giggling, the two ladies trying to dress and put Bhutun on board, this was our daily show.

I have lost touch with them but I have heard that the little boy is now a famous lawyer in town. Wow.

Ani, do you remember how slim you were and how Masi was constantly trying to fatten you up with milk sweets, biscuits, anything and everything she possibly could get you to eat but all you did was nibble and you stayed slim.

I miss our childhood so much.

Do you remember the large whitewashed house next to ours? It looked like it was a few houses down only because it was such a big house that it went on for some time if you walked down from our house. The house was cool clean and I loved the people who lived in it, it was Minniepisi and Didan, Minniepisi's mum. Minniepisi was pretty in a homely kind of way and the fact that she worked and lived with her mum and was not married was great, it meant they both had tons of time for me. So I would go over to their house in the weekends when Minniepisi was not working, I would get busy sketching, making paper boats and play with her long dark hair for hours. She never once lost her patience with me, always sweet and kind, and Didan would bring us goodies like semolina kheer which I loved.

The prayer room in their house was a tunnel and I remember the adults had to half crawl to get in, though once you were in, it was shiny clean and fragrant with flowers and incense. I loved sitting inside, especially on a hot day.

Remember Anita, Minniepisi later marrying my uncle's close friend? I was happy for her but after the marriage, she moved and we never met. I would love to meet her and talk about old times and how she let a bored little girl play with her tresses.

It was a tight little community, ours, just five or six families. We knew everything about each other and were there for each other. Do you remember when we first moved Ani when my dad was transferred and we all went to live with him? I was so excited then at the prospect of travelling but as time has gone on, I have missed our little para more and more. I wish I had never left.

Molly woke up, drenched in sweat, her heart beating a million times a minute. The result of looking through some old albums she found while trying to clear the attic. So there she was writing a letter to her old childhood friend from Kolkata, someone she had not seen or spoken to for years. It was difficult to know what to do with old pictures.

As a young girl, Molly loved what is called psychometric testing, where you have to answer questions like what's your favourite kind of road? Or draw a river and a snake and a bicycle. She used to love doing this kind of stuff because it was fun and it was sometimes quite telling how two different people drew two completely different rivers and snakes and bicycles. Maybe she should have studied psychology, not medicine. That's definitely a thought.

Molly remembers being fantastic at Scrabble, so good that she could literally beat anybody and because nearly everybody knew, no one wanted to play with her. She remembered being utter rubbish at Monopoly; she was always broke—no money for rent, no houses on her properties and the like, again because nearly everybody knew nobody was interested.

Her grandma was a wizard at cards and she taught Molly a lot of card games like Fish, Queen of hearts, Bray and the like, these were popular then and because Molly was neither very good nor very bad, people did not mind playing with her. Phew, this was a happy medium desperately needed for the long summer holidays.

The card games from her childhood surfaced again when Molly was in medical school after their final exams and she taught her class mates how to play bridge, and they spent long hours playing and even longer hours fighting over it because they had finished their exams and were now working as interns in the hospital.

That time, after the final exams, they also had a magazine club, the side effect of no further exams and also the fact that they were now interns earning money.

The first time that she got paid, Molly was over the moon, her first salary at age 23, it was such a fantastic thing that it was difficult to compare it with anything else.

It was a princely sum of 923 rupees and you needed to buy special stamps from the post office for this purpose. Molly remembered her mum telling her that these stamps cost many thousands of rupees so when she heard that she had to buy stamps, she was in despair how she can buy stamps worth thousands of rupees when her salary was 923 rupees? This stopped her from collecting her salary until she was dragged to the post office by her classmates who were also collecting their first salaries. There she saw that the stamp was definitely not the one her mum had mentioned, it cost a few pennies, thank God.

But then she was such a spender, she would be broke in two weeks flat, no wonder she was such a rubbish monopoly player, and then spent the next two weeks waiting for her next payday.

But it was great because her hostel was in a semi-rural area and things were far more affordable than a city. Molly's school friends who had qualified from hospitals in large urban areas still had to accept money from their parents as the 923 rupees would not take you very far in a big city. Molly loved treating her classmates and once every couple of months they would cook and eat together, luchi (fried bread) and chicken curry almost always. Once they had bought some shrimps but the shrimp smelt so terrible that Molly was about to bin the shrimp thinking it must've gone off. Her old roomie appeared by pure chance and stopped her at the nick of time, it seems all shrimp smells like that and it hadn't gone off at all.

The first few months of joining medical school were at once terrifying and exhilarating. The prospect of Molly leaving home and living independently was mostly terrifying for her mum but for her it was terrifying and exhilarating in equal measure. She had never handled money except for paying bus fares or buying street food before and now she had to live on a certain sum of money every month. It was scary having to decide everything: when do you decide to wash your clothes? When do you decide to go and buy groceries? There was nobody to ask because though the senior girls were very supportive, they were up to their eyes in studies and exams.

Molly had been thrown in at the deep end and she was paddling furiously to stay afloat. Not all her new friends were like her, some were really grown up and managed everything really well and there were others like her who just somehow bumbled along.

When they first joined, the college threw them a fresher's welcome programme followed soon enough by the college annual programme and this was followed by a programme at a reputed local college to which they were all invited.

Molly and a small group of her class friends were asked to sing for the fresher's, the annual programme and of course the one to which they were invited. They performed as part of the college group with a few senior members who either sang or accompanied them on stage. Molly loved performing; she was not nervous at all and because they were in a group it was great fun.

The college ones were within the campus but the one outside the campus that the local college invited them to perform was an adventure. In her heart, she knew that she was a first year student but there was no harm in pretending she was a real artist that was fancy all right. During the course of the rehearsals, she met quite a few seniors—boys and girls who sang and performed in the college band. The girls were a friendly bunch and the boys were polite and that suited Molly just fine. One of the older boys had qualified but came to teach them some songs in between working at the hospital and also to rehearse with them as he was very musical and very committed.

This older boy, Dr Sen, always drew a plan of the stage for each programme indicating where they would stand. Molly noticed to her surprise that according to this plan, her position was nearly always right next to him.

That's probably because I am petite, nothing else.

However, after the local college function all the other girls were asking Dr Sen to take them out for a drink (not alcohol, Thums Up) and to Molly's great surprise, Dr Sen came and asked her if she would like a cold drink. Molly agreed, still wondering why he was asking her when he could go out with nearly every other girl in college.

It was a beautiful evening, the weather was cool and they took their drinks to sit outside where they could see the twinkling lights of the town centre. It was the kind of beautiful evening that only happens when you are nineteen years old and you are having your first cold drink with a boy, and you feel happy and excited.

Molly remembered she had to go home on the night train the next day, it was strange she did not want to go and as if in keeping with this she could not find her tickets when she reached the station. Dr Sen had accompanied her to the station and it was very embarrassing for Molly when he bought her a train ticket, Molly tried to say thank you but he said, "Be careful, don't lose this again" in a tone so familiar that it shocked Molly. What was that about?

Once she reached home, Molly was so happy to see her parents and younger brother that college seemed distant, even unreal sometimes. It was only a short break and she was soon back, attending lectures making notes preparing for semesters.

She had been a late riser and a night owl all her life till then but here she tried setting her alarm and waking up early in the morning to start reading *Grey's Anatomy*.

Anatomy is the first subject one usually reads with physiology and biochemistry following shortly after but Molly found most of her friends just memorising the facts.

She was struggling to acquire a concept of anatomy of the groin area as that is usually the first chapter called Femoral Triangle. To this day she does not remember how it came about but in a few days she found herself sitting in the library with Dr Sen, a huge anatomy atlas open between them on the initial chapter, the Femoral Triangle.

It was awkward there being just the two of them in the library and the topic he was trying to teach her even more so. Molly felt so conscious of herself that she could not concentrate. She made her excuses and left the library as soon as she could.

The real surprise came when Molly least expected it. You might say this was not a surprise at all, in hindsight it probably was expected, but at the time it fell on Molly like a bombshell. A letter given to her by Dr Sen after she came back from a weekend at home with family saying she was like an oasis in his life, that he could not live without her and his life depended on her from now, etc., etc.

Oh my God, such a lot of drama, so this was why he wanted to have Thums Up with me and he bought my rail ticket too, it all made sense.

Molly was quite direct, she told Dr Sen she did not love him like that and she did not want to marry him or anyone else at all. It is important to be honest always.

When Dr Sen heard Molly's reply, he looked really hurt but he kept writing, kept asking her out, kept telling her how pretty she was. He worked away at her refusal and Molly felt herself softening slowly. He is a nice guy, from a very different background no doubt but he really loves me. And all the other girls just adored him.

Once Molly's parents were visiting her and Dr Sen came and said hello to them and when she saw them talking together, Molly felt this looked right, that Dr Sen would fit in with her family.

When she told him after her parents had left, he cried rather openly, she was about to say don't cry, when he popped in with, "Don't call me Dr Sen for god's sake, not anymore, call me Molloy."

"Ok, don't cry, Molly."

That marked the end of her adolescence and the beginning of her youth.

Chapter 3

Molly remembered settling into the front row seat of a British Airways flight from Dumdum to London Heathrow with her two-year-old daughter in the late 1990s.

As the plane started taxiing, she had the sinking realisation that all the other people would be coming back while hers was a one-way ticket, as the plane took off she felt this strange pain, it was as if her insides were being wrenched out, her roots being pulled out and twisted like weeds. The image of India that she carried in her heart then is the image she still carries today.

India on the other hand has undergone serious transformations in the last decade or so. Molly knows this in her head but her heart still yearns for the country she left behind in the1990s.

Getting to know fellow countrymen here, Molly felt we are all carrying our own little versions of the country we left behind. Every time we visit, we feel unsettled and in trying to get away from this, we have created here in our tiny expat world, a little India that does not really exist except in our conversations, in our gatherings and in our psyches.

We seek emotional shelter in it and revel in its glories, thinking, *yes, we still are truly Indian.* The truth is that we do not belong anywhere, in India we are NRIs, and here we are 'immigrants' at best.

The day I boarded that BA flight from Dumdum, I lost my country somehow, I did not know it then.

Like a superfine sword that splits you in two but you don't know this till the two halves fall away from each other. Like they have now.

Chapter 4

Molly's youth began with a mistake.

It was a mistake to agree to go out with Dr Sen, her studies were suffering and she knew how shocked her parents would be if they found out. It was a mistake to allow him to hold her hand but to her surprise, his hand was soft with long tapered fingers. She actually enjoyed talking to him holding his hand and they went for long walks in the country.

This led to certain problems as the girls hostel gates shut at 10 and opened at five all year round and the walks sometime ended after 10 pm and then she had to wake up the night guard. This was the pre mobile phone era so what seems really simple now like calling the guard was quite impossible then and became a difficulty. Not only was the front gate shut and the night guard fast asleep when Molly returned but the kitchen was also closed and there was no dinner for her. Not one to be put out by anything, Molly would usually swallow a few large spoonsful of powdered milk and then drink a few glasses of water. "It tastes delicious, I love milk powder and it will be morning soon anyway."

One of her seniors tried to scare her saying that large amounts of milk powder can cause intestinal obstruction—a traffic jam of the bowels usually remedied by emergency operation but that kind of thing never fazed Molly.

She merely found the information amusing.

It was around this time that once when Molly was home for the summer break that Dr Sen fell seriously ill. He was working in the gynae and obstetric wards then.

They used to write to each other every day, and Molly remembered waiting every afternoon till after lunch (sadly her mum never took a siesta like her friend's mums) and then tiptoeing downstairs in the searing heat to check the letterbox. It would be about 40deg Celsius then and the staircase of the community buildings they lived in would be deserted.

They lived on the fourth floor of a typical block of flats with no lifts and craggy cement stairs, the letter box was on the ground floor under the stairs. So, Molly came down four floors to get the letter and climbed up five floors to the terrace every day in 40 degrees plus but thought nothing of it then. The chubby envelope from Molloy more than made up for every hardship.

She was rewarded most days and she would go straight up to the terrace (likely 42deg) to read the letter in private.

Once when Dr Sen was visiting her, they had gone to the terrace for (Molly's parents being conservative, they asked him to come and visit her instead of meeting outside, hence the terrace) a bit of 'fresh air' that he touched her. This had never happened before and she bit into his collar and dug her face into his neck. Her body was trembling and exploding and explosion never felt so sweet. Her head was a bit swimmy when they came downstairs as Mum had called them down for tea (perfect timing), she hoped no one would notice.

When they were walking or sitting side by side, Molloy always insisted Molly stay on his left, it was a private joke that Molloy's left shoulder was designed particularly to hold Molly's head, therefore Molly should stay on his left. Funny thing to remember.

Another evening on the terrace, he wanted to kiss her but she was shy and resisted. She had never been kissed and felt it was going too far. But a few weeks into the summer, Dr Sen told her that he was not keeping well at all. In fact, he could not continue his internship and had been asked to go home, He had developed Hepatitis from needle injury and needed time and rest to recover before he could restart. In his present state, he was infectious so it was both for his benefit and for patient safety. Molly was worried out of her mind, she begged him to see her on his way home as there was nowhere else they could meet.

And nobody knew how long it would take him to recover. He only came for lunch (ma made chicken stew and rice served in fancy bowls, plain fare to help his digestion). He told Molly she looked very pretty and that he found it very hard to say bye.

Molly found it hard too, her eyes were welling up and there was a lump in her throat knowing she would not see him for weeks now. She still remembers the simple deep red cotton saree she wore that day, a Bandhni print from western India.

At the end of summer, Molly was looking forward to going back to college meeting all her friends and of course Dr Sen. She could not wait to see him and started having sneaking thoughts, *Am I in love? How do people know they are in love?*

It was great to be back, being free, being broke and all the rest but the best thing was she could see Dr Sen every day…well, nearly every day except when he was on take on a Wednesday and sometimes over weekends. By this time, they were going out together and Molly liked being with him. He was sweet, caring and very witty. But his reports were not clear and he needed more tests in a few months to check for the clearance of the infection.

Dr Sen told Molly he might still be carrying the virus, so…the funny thing is the fact that she should not kiss Dr Sen made her want to kiss him all the more and she fell on him every time they managed to be alone, which was not often, and tried to kiss him full on.

Dr Sen tried to stop her but gave in when Molly said she did not mind if she got Hepatitis too. Kissing him full on was super exciting because it was not the right thing to do on so many levels. Practice makes perfect and Molly soon became an expert kisser.

Molly's parents doted on her as their eldest and had great plans for her. They were visiting her at her hostel once over a long weekend when Dr Sen 'casually dropped by' to say hello. They spoke for a while and Molly remembers watching her parents and him talking and she felt they looked so good together like they really belonged, she knew she could be the missing link between them. That was the First Big Mistake.

Chapter 5

"Hey sexy."

"Hey?"

"What's a girl like you doing in a place like this?"

"Very funny."

"Come here and give me a big wet kiss.

"Across my dead body."

"Really, do I have to kill you for a kiss?"

"Get out, you silly duffer."

"After you, my sexy…"

Molly and Molloy, when they first met, were a red-hot couple, the envy of all the other couples in the uni campus. None of them could match their easy camaraderie and their fine sense of humour.

It came naturally to them, so they were quite literally the life and soul of every party they went to. When it was time to leave, the whole campus threw a big au revoir party for them. All the students, most of the teachers and even the Dean attended. It was talked about for months and years after as the best party the campus had seen in a long time.

The news that Molly and Molloy were not together anymore literally shook the place by its foundation, no one believed it at first, it was impossible they said. These were two people literally made for each other.

Molly remembers the first time Molloy saw her breasts; he went mad quite literally.

"I am going crazy, Molius, I want to touch them, feel them, kiss them, hold them, sleep with them, do everything with them, I am going crazy."

"What about me, Molloy," she had said but he was not listening to her.

Their first night together happened quite accidentally at a friend's birthday party. It was a warm Saturday in August when Maggie asked them and a few others over for a barbecue at her new place. It was a cosy house but the garden was generous and the barbecue went off fabulously.

By the end of the evening, none of them were fit to walk let alone drive home and Maggie being the superb host brought out all her bedding and sleeping bags to try and settle her friends. Maggie was single and had only moved into the new house a fortnight back, so the bedding in spite of her best efforts was in short supply.

After settling everyone as best as she could, bless her there was only one large sleeping bag left and she asked if Molly and Molly could share.

Molly still blames Maggie for what happened next.

Born in a conservative family, educated in a convent, Molly's view of sex was completely Victorian. She viewed sex as something that was necessary in order to have children and there ended the matter. It was never discussed or talked about at home or among friends. She had never seen her parents kissing or hugging and was shocked when she saw her friends' parents being openly affectionate.

But that was them and this was her, there was no reason for her to be like them anymore than they had reason to be like her.

But once inside the sleeping bag, her body started behaving strangely and she could not make it listen to her brain anymore. It seemed to take on a life of its own.

Molloy started kissing her neck and squeezing her, she tried to resist him but her body was not listening to her. They soon came together and Molloy was whispering sweet nothings in her ear.

They fell asleep after that but woke up at dawn and made love again. This time it was slower, more mature and more electric and Molly remembered crying her eyes out after. Molloy was puzzled to see her crying. "Have I hurt you, sweetie? Why are you crying?"

Molly was crying with happiness but she didn't know how to explain that to Molloy, she remembered her friends discussing how men did not understand these feelings, so she just kissed him saying she was fine.

Chapter 6

Molly was running into a forest, she wanted to stop but an invisible hand was pushing her forward, the forest grew deeper and darker and the trees closed in on her, scratching her face and clothes and tearing her hair. *I have to stop,* thought Molly, stumbling forward through the dense forest, why can't I stop? Suddenly, she found herself in a large clearing, *I will stop now,* thought Molly. By this time, she had reached the edge of the clearing and now the giant hand was pushing her off the edge of the clearing, deep into the abyss of darkness.

She woke up drenched in sweat, shaking like a leaf, in her bedroom. *I have to see somebody,* thought Molly; these nightmares have been going on and she has been unable to stop them.

It was hard and it kept on getting harder to 'run all night in the forest' and then go to work in the morning as if nothing had happened, as if she had slept like everyone else.

Her tired eyes and ever widening dark circles invited questions from colleagues and team members that she could do without. She could not tell them about her nightmares and they put it down to things she didn't have in her life.

I have to get up now or I will be late for work, thought Molly; she quickly showered made a brew and was in the car in about fifteen minutes. She did not wear makeup and the strict dress code at work was a boon in disguise, there was her usual uniform and security fob round her neck and that was that. *No time wasted thinking about what to wear, what accessories, etc., Molly liked it like this, less hassle,* she thought.

Work had been a saviour for Molly, it kept her sane and grounded and of course paid her bills and the lawyer's fees which were heavy to say the least.

A few of her friends had gathered around and protected her from the elements and without their support, Molly would probably be not here at all. She had tried to take her own life and when she could not succeed had instead thought of approaching Dignitas for euthanasia. She had thought of this as a painless solution to her problems and was disappointed when she found out that in order to get help from Dignitas, one had to have proof of an incurable illness. I *do have an incurable illness,* thought Molly, *but it will not be on the Dignitas list of incurable illnesses sadly.*

She entered her room at work to find that the cleaner was still in there, cleaning her room, *oh no*, thought Molly, now she would have to find all her papers and arrange her equipment all over again.

Molly had to have her whole room set up before she started clinic to ensure she did not waste time looking for any equipment, everything was laid out systematically.

The cleaner was known for her missionary zeal for arranging things and tidying up, *I hope she doesn't put me in one of her orange bins,* thought Molly.

"Hi Mols, good morning."

"Good morning Anna, how was your weekend?"

"Oh Peter was sick again and we had to take him to the vet, did not sleep a wink all night."

"Oh no, what happened?"

"The vet thinks he has gastritis, he is on medicines the poor bugger."

"I bet the vets bills are steep too Anna, and Nigel didn't sleep either?"

"You are joking, Mols he was snoring before I even came back from the vet, that's men for you, the selfish bastards."

"He must've been tired, Anna, he works hard you said that yourself."

"Well, yes but I work hard too, just taken on an extra shift this week."

"I know what you mean, let's hope you get some sleep tonight."

"Yeah see you around."

Molly had a busy day at work, one of those days when you do not have a minute and at the end of the day wonder where the time has gone. *Oh this is good; I will sleep tonight,* thought Molly, she remembered how she used to sleep as a student in school and uni how her parents were always joking that if there was a tsunami, she would sleep straight through it.

Some of her friends took sleepers but she felt that if the body needed sleep, the body would sleep by itself no chemicals needed, the problem of course was that Molly was so tense and anxious when she went to bed that she ended up staying awake all night and then dozing off around dawn. So really, she only got proper rest over weekends.

Molly desperately wanted to sleep, but of course sleep was not easy, and it has not been for a very long time.

Chapter 7

Molly loves watching Bollywood when she is home sick, she misses the sights sounds and the noises of her big dusty noisy beautiful country. Every Bollywood film true to its bling will have a marriage as its central theme. This is understandable, it's the best excuse for songs and dances and colours and dresses and pretty girls and all the rest of what makes a hit film.

Molly was the only girl on her side of the family and the oldest amongst her cousins so when she completed her graduation, there was talk in the family about her marriage. She had been seeing Molloy for the last six years by then and the family knew of this unofficially.

Her dad was not much in favour of her getting married because he felt that marriage would distract her, she would miss out on her post-graduation and will not study after she got married.

Molly tried to convince her parents, brazen as that sounds now it is true, she was very eager to get married, marriage seemed like the best thing to happen to her, she had waited so long and she was conscious that her husband-to-be was also waiting. How could anyone be so naive?

Molloy's parents came to their flat in Kolkata on an autumn evening. A small feast was laid out for them, Molly's mum asked her to wear a saree and Molloy sat quietly in a corner as the dutiful son looking like someone who had been dragged in against his will.

The evening went off okay and after Molly's dad and brother had returned to the house after seeing them off, everyone sat down to discuss what was going to happen next, as the marriage was now officially on.

The marriage scene in Calcutta is always busy and booming and the idea is that if you want to get married, you have to hire the venue first, the only thing that comes before the venue is the groom, so once you have the groom/bride, you hire the venue because if you don't, you will not be able to get married as venues get taken very quickly.

Luckily, Molly's uncle lived in a lovely old house sat on spacious gardens so this was the automatic choice of venue, everyone agreed, nobody wanted to go hunting for venues, that was a nightmare.

The preparation started a few months before the wedding, the whole house was painted and redecorated.

Molly's dad who never took interest in anything remotely domestic had some German catalogues brought in for Molly's furniture; he then consulted a special carpenter and brought the wood for the carpenter to make the furniture in one of the empty rooms in Molly's uncle's house. He also took a real interest in Molly's jewellery; her mum was beyond surprised. There was great excitement in the family as all the cousins were really young and this was the first big family wedding coming up. Astrologers from both sides of the family met up to discuss dates and the date was fixed in winter which is also the best season to get married back home. Molly was an intern in paediatrics and she had a sincere hard-working senior so she had to work equally hard.

Molly liked hands-on work so she enjoyed every minute and paediatrics was her favourite specialty to this day.

The only problem was that the hospital had very little equipment say, for example, one day they ran out of saline bottles and if a child came in with dehydration they could not start a drip. If a child needed treatment after dark, the lights were so dim that all the doctors had to carry powerful torches but this of course had to be held by someone while you did the procedure. When you are learning, this makes it much more challenging. The other reason they all carried torches was that the area around the hostel was known to have snakes, especially in summer.

So it was as much for themselves as for patients that they all carried long and powerful torches in those days.

There was little time to go downtown to make a phone call so Molly would write a postcard each week to her parents just stating that she was well. Her mum replied and wrote back saying all the preparations were going forward and she needed to apply for leave in good time.

All of Molly's hostel mates were excited though sadly very few could attend because of work and because they would have to travel to Kolkata to attend.

Molly arrived home two days before the wedding, her mum took one look at her dishevelled hair and dark circles and she was carted straight off to the beautician for head to toe work. She wanted to say, 'let me sleep, I will look fine', but no one was listening. She was scrubbed and polished and fed for two days then the festivities started.

All the men and the boys in the family wanted a haircut so someone had the brilliant idea of asking a barber from a local men's salon to come with his equipment. When told of the number of clients waiting, the barber readily agreed and Molly still remembers looking out of the window in her uncles house to see a little makeshift salon under a large tree in the garden and her cousins and uncles all waiting in queue for a haircut, all on the house, of course.

Do such things happen anymore? No idea.

There was a professional cook coming every day because there were about thirty to forty people to cook for twice daily on a regular basis. Mum and the senior aunts managed the pantry and Dad and uncles did the shopping. It was all so well organised, no one would believe this was our first big family wedding.

For the days of the wedding, one of Molly's dad's friends who owned a lovely nursery in the suburbs offered to decorate the house with flowering plants and everyone marvelled at the effect of fresh flowering plants throughout the house, it made everything look so beautiful. By now, the furniture was made and the carpenter had left with a smile and it was all decked out in fancy covers.

On the day of the wedding, Molly's mum woke her up at dawn and asked her to eat some sweet yoghurt, she had no idea what this was about and was too sleepy to ask. So, she gulped it down dutifully and went back to sleep. The religious ceremonies were sombre but the rest of the day was fun. Molly was supposed to be fasting but her cousins kept slipping her food so she was fine really. She had heard of other brides passing out because of fasting, she did not want any of that drama, thank you.

A lady came in the afternoon to do her makeup, hair, etc., she was superefficient; she did the whole getup in less than an hour. Molly still had pictures of this beautician doing her face and hair, strange how some pictures stay while others get lost in the sands of time.

For the wedding day, her parents had chosen a very fancy catering service and they served French cuisine—difficult to pronounce but who cares? It was delicious and got great feedback from the guests.

Molly found the main wedding ceremony quite stressful because it went on for a long time and the combined heat from the holy fire and the video lights was difficult when you are wearing a heavy saree and so much jewellery. It was lovely to just sit down and rest with friends and family after the ceremony and Molly and Molloy were allowed to talk to each other among a group of friends.

Molly could see the senior team of Mum-Dad-aunts-uncles relieved everything had gone off smoothly so they could relax now. Her cousins and friends were having a great time partying and singing.

It was a beautiful night, better than any Bollywood wedding Molly had seen.

Chapter 8

We as a generation seem to have forgotten how to talk to our children, it's almost as if we are guilty. Guilty of being ourselves?

The other day, Molly was trying to concentrate on the patient's problem while his little girl was jumping up and down on the weighing scales, making a lot of noise. She was worried about missing something and of course the scales might break. So she asked the little girl not to jump and sit down next to her dad.

To her utter shock, Dad turned to the little girl and said, "I will buy you one when we get home."

Molly was so surprised at this response that she said, "You know, it's okay to tell your child there are some things they cannot do." No response from Dad who clearly thought Molly was some kind of living fossil.

After this incident, she requested accompanying children to sit in the waiting area but that was not always feasible. The children might be very young coming in with Mum who had come to consult with Molly.

So Molly had to steel herself internally to listen to Mum while a child might be screaming at the top of their lungs or pulling every drawer open to rummage inside. She had once requested a patient to try and calm her child down so Molly could concentrate on the patient's problem but the patient turned around and said, "You have to do this, I cannot help you."

The sound of a child's cry used to unsettle Molly completely and it took her a lot of time and effort to be able to focus on the problem at hand with a child crying/screaming in the background. It still took a lot out of her.

This was a country where children were supposed to be seen and not heard and by a strange turn of events, our children are exactly that nowadays because their heads are always buried in some or the other screen. Also children in Victorian England were not allowed to sit at the dining table, they had to stand and eat and usually only had leftovers which resulted in widespread malnourishment and sickness.

Maybe we are trying to deny the past and in a great rush to appear fair and modern we have now labelled all parental intervention as abuse. Where does that leave the children, I wonder, with no directions from parents.

A ship without a radar is bound to run aground.

Some parents are so worried of doing or saying the wrong things or have so little time for their children that the children do not get any guidance at all. What sort of parents will these children become?

Chapter 9

It is strange how childish Molly is in spite of her years and her life experiences. Her innocence keeps her young and hopeful and everyone who meets her says, 'wow, you are so bubbly and funny'.

Molly likes it like that, better to die laughing than crying, she always thought. Why weigh people down with her worries? Surely, they have enough of their own, why not try to cheer them? Lift them up a little bit even for two minutes, make them feel happy and confident in their own skin.

She thinks it is important, especially as a doctor, as most patients tend to think that as a doctor she is not on their side, maybe because they expect the doctor to be on a different socioeconomic level and therefore not one of them.

Mol has always tried to share with patients that she too is exhausted after a long day at work, she too loves shopping and going out, she too is struggling to lose weight.

But then this is very risky.

So the moment she has a laugh with the patient and the consultation becomes a friendly exchange, the patient starts asking for favours only because they don't want to ring and make another appointment.

So on the one hand it is great to laugh with the patient and make things convivial but the problem is that the patient will immediately start asking for her mum's blood reports, her son's creams, her husband's tablets—the list is never-ending. So, this is why some doctors will try their best to keep things very professional so they can keep to the times allotted to each patient and not get bogged down with extra favours and requests. That is totally understandable.

Mol however has a different take on this, for one thing she enjoys a laugh as it helps relieve stress, and two, she believes that if she can save the patients time by doing the requests because the patient would have rung and made another apt anyway, then she is saving time all round maybe not hers but everyone else and patients love her for this.

Many of her patients when she rang them would ask her how she was and say how long they had waited to book an appointment, especially with her. This did not make her feel special at all. It made her feel guilty that patients have waited so long and also awkward she did not quite know what to say to this.

Was it a compliment? Was it a complaint? Was it a comment?

It was a complex and confusing area.

But thankfully, not everything is complex and confusing. Molly was leaving work on a Friday in the midst of heavy rain when she noticed one of her elderly patients walking out of the practice with her.

"Hi Brenda, how are you?"

"Hi Doc, I was thinking about you, I had come to see the nurse for my jabs but I need to book an appointment with you next week."

"Not a problem, Brenda, but how are you going to get home?"

"Oh don't worry, I will walk."

"Not in this weather, let me drop you on my way, I know where you live, I have visited you during Covid, haven't I?"

"Oh, Dr, that is so good of you, what would you like; Royal Glacial mints or Time Off?"

"I would love Time Off please."

That's what she is like, always bringing chocolate and mints for everyone in the practice. Molly tried telling Brenda that it's dangerous to bring her chocolates but Brenda was not listening. Molly and Brenda laughed a lot in the car and then Molly dropped her off, waved her bye and came home feeling a million bucks.

GPs are asked not to socialise with patients but this was just helping her get home, nothing more. That reminded Molly of another patient, a young girl who keeps asking Molly to have coffee with her. Molly has tried telling the patient that it's against the rules to socialise with patients but that fell on deaf ears.

This was months ago but the patient did not forget, whenever she comes, she reminds Molly, "Dr, when are we going for coffee?"

"You know I am not supposed to have coffee with patients."

"It's only coffee, please Doctor." "I will definitely try next week."

Molly felt bad doing this but breaking rules was not a good idea. From breaking one rule to another and then down a slippery slope, hope not.

Best to be extra careful because if anyone sees and reports her, then as an Asian doctor, she will be judged far more harshly than her Caucasian counterparts.

Chapter 10

It was a beautiful Sunday morning in January and the weather was awesome, it was clear and bright with deep blue skies fluffy white clouds and you could see for miles.

It's perfect, I better take Alfie for his walk now.

Mol got ready in a jiffy and Alfie was very excited at the prospect of a walk. He knew she would let him run loose in the fields, sniff all the grass and posts, say hello to all other dogs and kids…the list was endless but Molly enjoyed his happiness and how can you be happy if you are not free? She did not like the dog walkers' style of walking Alfie, like an elephant in procession in a regal manner, bang in the middle of the road. Alf hated that, he loved the little grassy patches, the strange plants, the old wooden fence posts and all that's green and wet, generally speaking. Molly loved to see his excitement and put up with washing him after the walk which took nearly an hour, because you had to soap him then wash followed by towel dry and then hairdryer.

It was well worth his happiness and excitement.

Alf went through it all without a sound as if he somehow knew he had to. He was very good-natured, everyone said so including people who did not have to say anything like the postman, the estate agent and other visitors. Alf came to the house when he was eight weeks old and was a little furry bundle of mischief. He loved his food, enjoyed exploring around the house but he still ran behind the sofa when he saw the hoover. Mol had always known that dogs love going for walks so after his injections she bought his collar and tried to take him out one fine summer afternoon.

That was a disaster if ever there was one. He stood with his feet firmly planted on the ground and after about half an hour of trying to get him to walk next to her, she had no choice but to pick him up and go for a quick round with him in her arms. He was quite comfortable when he was in her arms but he did not want to be put on the ground. So, the walk lasted a measly fifteen minutes.

He is now nearly two years and he has changed so much that he becomes dizzy with excitement as soon as Mol puts his harness on.

Once at the door he starts barking and running and has to be controlled then. So, he is on leash initially but as he settles into the walk and they walk out of the estate into the wood's Molly can finally unleash him. When she unleashes him, Mol usually says stop, opens the latch and says go. He runs like the wind then, ears flapping in the breeze, tail upright like a flag, Molly enjoys his excitement sooo much.

To anyone who has not had a dog, it is very difficult to explain what it is like to have one. A dog can love you like no human being ever can. Mol often told her friends that we should all aspire to love each other like dogs do, totally unconditional and selfless. No human being, no matter how much they love you, can just sit next to you all the time but a dog does just that and amazingly too.

Molly was a dog person and always wanted one but Molloy was a cat person so she agreed to have a cat for him. The cat was very well behaved and loved Molly because she brought him treats all the time.

Molly agreed that there are dog lovers and cat lovers but at the end of the day, your pet is a member of your family and that's the most important thing.

Chapter 11

The days are growing shorter and the nights longer and darker. The super happy TV presenter who smiles brighter than the sun at mid-day on the equator tells Molly each day that this is the mildest November on record but it's hard to believe. Molly would have liked a clear crisp cold November rather than a wet cloudy muggy November if that's what mild means nowadays.

Molly waits and waits and waits to see her children, even a hello on the phone or a Hi on text can make her day. But week after week of no contact at all makes her desperate and low. She keeps ringing and texting them to say hello, to hear their voice but there is never any response, none at all.

So the long dark nights and the short-wet days do not help at all. But we all change with time and Molly feels she has grown slow and careful with time. It's as if she does not trust her arms and legs to respond as swiftly or she thinks her eyes will take longer to see and react. Maybe it is true.

While driving back after a long day at work, she usually listens to light music on the radio as she cannot listen to serious discussions at that point and music tends to cheer her up too. This is the time she misses her children the most.

She remembers when the children lived with her she would go home and make dinner for them. She loved Wednesdays because that used to be her day off so she would wait for the kids to come home and would always plan a special dish for her family.

She remembers buying basil for pasta until one day her daughter said—why basil, Mum, just use coriander. It had never occurred to her to use fresh coriander in pasta but then she did not bother with basil anymore. The kids loved roast lamb and vegetables with rosemary but that was usually for Christmas. The amount of rosemary she used was a standing joke. Every guest had a little rosemary bush on their plate. Molly knew that to get the favour of the herb, you had to use a certain amount and as long as her dinner guests cleaned their plates she did not mind the jokes about the herb garden, they loved the roast with red wine and rosemary and veggies with cheese sauce.

She was driving home and all these thoughts were going through her mind. She had the radio on to distract her from exactly these thoughts as they made her cry and driving while crying is both unsafe and unsavoury. Molly stopped at a pedestrian crossing and saw the cutest little boy wearing a bright red coat crossing the road with his mum.

No amount of pop music could hold her tears after that, she did not try to stop them either. Better out than in. The same thing happened when one of her patients kissed or cuddled their children during the consultation, Molly needed to summon all her professional strength to continue as if nothing had happened, while her heart was being ripped into shreds with longing for her children.

Most days Molly drove home after work through tears, its lucky she has never crashed her car.

The other day she was consulting with a teenager with his hair pulled low over his forehead trying his best to avoid eye contact, all her queries were met with a silence a grunt or a shrug so that after about ten minutes of questioning, Molly was none the wiser than when she started. Typical teenager, she thought and smiled, thinking that her son is also a teenager but his hair is brushed clean, he is polite and well-mannered. She had only been able to gloat for a few seconds before realising that for all his politeness, he does not pick up the phone when she calls him or respond when she texts him.

Molly dreams every year of getting a card, maybe even a small present for Mother's Day or her birthday from her children. There is never a card for any occasion. Going into the card store for someone's card, she would look at the pretty gifts and cards for Mother's Day and think maybe she will get one this year.

Molly is sure that if the children lived with her, she would get them cards to give their dad for birthdays, etc. but she was not so lucky herself. She would have read the card a million times and treasured it if she ever got one. Once, in her desperation, Molly had thought maybe if I have cancer, my children will come and see me. But how can one get cancer? She can't will it or wish it on herself.

When she mentioned this to two of her closest friends, they said yes you silly goat you will be suffering and they might, mind you, just might send you a card...don't be foolish. Go and live your own life, they said.

And that was the end of Molly's cancer plan.

Chapter 12

Molly would love to call it a eureka moment but really that would be pushing it a bit.

It was a warm day and she was trying to tidy the kitchen when she came across a large glass jar full of peanuts in one of the back cupboards in her kitchen.

She had seen that jar before and those peanuts had been sitting there in their shell from the time of the Spanish Inquisition. *Let's shell them and if the nuts are still okay, I will fry them and keep them aside for garnish,* Molly thought.

When you open a peanut shell, you press with your thumb on a specific part on one end of the nut, that's the easy way but obviously if you are super strong, it does not matter—you can press anywhere.

While she was trying to crack peanut shells after what must have been at least two decades, Molly's mind took her back a few decades to life in medical school.

She had just started seeing her ex and they would go to movies together, not because the movies were good, simply because there was nowhere else to go and the movie hall was a nice place to sit next to each other, have peanuts with chilli salt and talk in between the scenes and at interval. It was not like Kolkata at all, no one ate popcorn or ice cream or drank fizzy cola here. It was usually tea, potato chips and peanuts.

Money was in seriously short supply as with all students so we stuck to peanuts—cheap, warm and tasty. They also had tea sometimes but that was after the film, usually with sweets and samosas. That was 'eating out', it was so much fun.

Before you ask, Molly has nothing against couples who snog in the back seats but they never did that.

Molly remembers the peanuts back then as being small and very hard, kind of gnarled, not the best quality one would assume and she always struggled to crack the shell. But someone had noticed she was struggling as he reached out and took the pack of peanuts from her hand and then proceeded to crack the shells and even put the nuts in her mouth. People around them were staring hard at them by now so they agreed that he will just crack the shells and pass the nuts, just that. Please do not feed the animals as they say.

In her kitchen however, faced with the same problem many decades later, it seemed a doddle. The shells were large and dry so Molly could locate the exact spot where she needed to press to crack the shells and hey-ho, she had shelled all the peanuts in no time at all.

Funnily enough, the nuts had not gone off so Molly proceeded to fry them and keep them aside as a good housewife should.

Any idea why the peanuts were so hard to crack then when she was about 19 as compared to now when she is 52?

Molly puts it down to experience.

Chapter 13

It's four in the morning and dark and stormy outside. Molly woke up, looking at the swaying trees and the leaves making a swishing noise. It was not scary at all; it was strangely comforting. After sometime, it was very still; the trees were standing in rapt attention as if waiting for an inspection. This happens just before the sun comes out, the trees standing still for the master to appear on the stage and for today's drama to be played out.

Molly packs so much into her days but somehow cannot escape the feeling of living in a vacuum. Everything is empty and superficial. How right the great Bard was when he said life is a stage. No truer word was ever said. However she still has to do everything that she has to do, no point telling your teacher that you did not do your homework because it's all a stage anyway. You risk serious telling off then.

When Molly tried to grasp the fact that only God is real, it gave her a strange assurance that somehow all the good and bad things, mostly bad things that are happening all around us are not real. They are like a film played on the screen of life. We are all part of this grand film so why not play her own role as well as possible. When Molly misses her children and the pain is difficult to bear, then she thinks they are her and she is them and that makes it a little less painful.

People look at her and Molly can see them thinking, *what did this woman do to her children? Why don't they want to see her? She looks okay but...*To this day, Molly wishes she knew the answer, she has gone through everything, every word, every conversation but she does not know why her own flesh and blood do not want her anymore. She has cried, begged, pleaded and apologised a million times, to no avail.

Were it not for work and meditation, Molly would have gone back to her old self-harming and drinking-herself-to-a-stupor to try to deal with the pain. And then of course the wise people in society would have turned around and said—we told you, she is a violent and unstable person, that is why the children do not wish to see her, maybe it's their meticulous planning that had made Molly behave in that manner in the past.

She was young and foolish then; she is old and foolish now.

Chapter 14

To my daughter: Hi sweetie,

Thinking of you a lot today; maybe you also are thinking of me. I'm working in a practice with a lot of children's toys in the room. Most practices do not have toys anymore due to problems with infection control but this one has plenty of old toys.

There are quite a few of the wooden ones that Molly loved.

I remember you had a fantastic selection of Barbie dolls as was the trend in those days.

Before that, you were obsessed with the Teletubbies, you would not eat without either them or the railway cartoons, I cannot remember the name but it had James the red engine. I know now it's Thomas the Tank Engine; that was when you were about three and this was the only thing we saw on television, I still remember the fat controller who always had jam sandwiches for tea and the voice of Ringo Starr in the background; yes, the Ringo Starr from Beatles.

Those were fun days, I was not working then because I still needed to do my exams and you had not started school so we spent a lot of time together.

Molly would not have passed without Molloy's help; he was an excellent teacher.

Teaching, you see dearie, is not the same as learning so good students don't make good teachers, not necessarily.

Molly thinks with teachers it's more about the skilled transfer of knowledge than just being a good student.

I think you would make a great teacher too, my sweetie pie, as you have excellent communication skills. I never thought I would be any good but I have been helping medicine and pharmacy students at our practice and it is alright.

From the fat controller and his jam sandwiches to teaching.

Do you remember I used to go to your school to wrap sarees on the girls in your year? This went on for a couple of years before the boys said they wanted something too, so from the next year, I used to take sarees for the girls and dhotis for the boys and everyone was happy.

It made me very happy to do something different, to make all the little boys and girls smile and jump with joy, it was so special.

Wonder where your school-friends are, probably at home given the current pandemic. I remember quite a few of your friends. I remember one little boy whose elder brother was studying to be dentist and I remember the pretty girl whose Dad was a GP.

We always invited the whole class for your birthday, it was great fun and you loved the partying same as I did. I remember we had your birthday parties at McDonalds and invited the whole class until you were about 12. And then you said I can't really go to McDonalds next year, Mum. That is when the parties got smaller and we stopped going to

McDonalds for birthday parties. I remember we used to have a bin bag in the car as that was the only way we could bring back all the presents.

You know, my sweetie, I have been reading quite a bit because really, how much television can one watch? I start getting headaches and my eyes start hurting after about three to four hours. I need to go away and rest my eyes.

And can you see how bad my writing is now, it is really terrible. I cannot believe it, I used to be proud of my writing in the past, I suppose I don't write enough. None of us write anymore, all those hours of cursive writing, what a waste. Little did we know then that we will not use pen and paper anymore.

As I was saying, the toys in the consulting room brought back a flood of memories. I remembered a store called the Early Learning Centre (probably gone now); it was my favourite but the one we visited most was Toys R Us (wondered if that is gone too).

Do you remember the big children's store in town? It was called Rosie and Jim, we used to go there for your birthday just before the day every year for your frock. I always bought pretty frocks for you for birthdays; when I was little, my mum used to buy my frock from a place called Little Shop, it is still there near Newmarket; you can check it out next time you visit India.

Do you still eat fuchka when you visit Kolkata?

I remember we always went during the summer holidays when it's really hot and humid.

Once we were out and though the car was air-conditioned, you were struggling with the heat and humidity but the minute I suggested fuchka, you agreed happily and your restlessness disappeared in a few seconds. Molly was so happy that her daughter loved street food as much as she did. I remember you loved fuchka and hajmola, it is difficult to love something you haven't grown up with or been born to but maybe your parents genes were playing out.

I hope you are not bored by this long letter, maybe you like this little trip down memory lane?

One day when you will be a mother you can tell your kids all about this funny food called fuchka and this yummy tablet called Hajmola.

Life goes on, my dear, look after yourself and everyone else. I know you are a very caring and affectionate person, sending you lots of love and hugs.

Maa.

Chapter 15

Molly is one of those people, always jotting down stuff, so if she goes somewhere, meets somebody, does something or even plans to do something and if she is looking forward to it, she will make notes.

These have stood her in good stead so now she can look back and see exactly what happened because our memories are biased for a reason. We try and forget things that hurt us because to remember everything would be horrible, was it Audrey Hepburn or Marilyn Monroe or Sophia Loren, never mind who, said that for a good life, we need good health and bad memory. While in the initial stages of divorce, Molly's ex would not allow her to get a lawyer, he said they do nothing and charge huge sums of money. When she said she really wanted one, he replied why should a lawyer come between us?

Molly has always been very emotional and could not bring herself to say that the whole world is between us now and what difference would one lawyer make? The fact was that she had known him since she was 18 and that he always called the shots and Molly agreed from habit. She still did not understand that her best friend of more than 25 years was now more or less her worst enemy.

So of course, Molly listened as she always did and they got a cheap online divorce where she never actually saw a lawyer.

She found out later that he had discussed the situation with several colleagues and they had all said that if he got a lawyer, everything would go to her. So that's why no lawyer could come between them.

After the divorce, they agreed to look after the children 50-50.

Molly hated the idea of taking the children away from their dad and from the big comfy house they knew as home as she had seen in a lot of her divorced colleagues.

Even when she was going to court to see her children, she came across quite a few women who did not let the children see their dad, that was so unfair on the children, how a mum could do that to her own children, she wondered.

She also could not stay in the marital home both financially and psychologically so she took a flat near the house and would have the children with her half the week and her ex would have them half the week; this went very well until he got married.

Then things started to fall apart. This happened slowly until Molly remembers coming back from seeing her parents in India and then taking the children to a social gathering for Holi and them being very quiet all the time they were there and after she dropped them off, Molloy rang to say that something had happened before she left, they had reported her to the social workers and that the social workers will be in touch.

If somebody had planned to take her children away from her, they could not have done it better. Following this, Molly was subjected to a lot of checks, questionnaires and had no contact with her children for a few years while she went to court and devoted all her time and energy to making more money to give to the lawyers.

There was a time when she couldn't afford a lawyer so spoke for herself in court, this was very stressful but she could've done anything to see her children.

She did not know about the legalities of divorce and custody then and this was a very steep curve for her.

She remembers meeting her first social worker.

This was in a large empty room, before Covid; she was sitting about 10 feet away, facing the window with her side towards her and she spoke without looking and Molly could tell that this wasn't going well.

She answered all the questions but really was not surprised to find that she had found her answers inadequate and that she would not give Molly access to her own children. Her body language at the interview had told Molly that she was totally biased to begin with.

Molly was upset but not daunted by this so she went to court again and studied the law in detail so she could discuss with her lawyers. She struggled for years going from one lawyer to another hoping they will be able to help her.

After about two years, she had an efficient and understanding social worker who listened and tried to understand the problem.

He tried to help me reconnect and Molly remembers meeting her children in Pizza Hut after two years of not seeing them at all. When she saw them, she started crying; she could feel the tears bubbling up from inside and she was shaking; her son kept very quiet, her daughter looked at her and said,

"What are you doing? Can you not see we are in a restaurant?" She was not happy or sad or excited, she was just very angry, her son was very embarrassed but maybe that was just his age. The court allowed Molly to see her children and gave her access every weekend after discussion with her ex and his lawyer.

Molly had moved to her new house which was nearly an hour's drive (her ex had said—don't live nearby, and foolishly, Molly listened again). Molly happily came every Saturday to pick them up, take them to hers for lunch or go somewhere for lunch and then drop them back, though the court had said they should take turns but the other side soon realised Molly would do it all to see her children so they let her drive for two hours to see her children for two hours, sometimes even less.

Even during the less than two hours, the children had constant texts from their dad who of course cared for them and was worried what Mum might be doing to them. You never know with these intellectual types, they are so unpredictable. They used to do this every Saturday as per court orders but as soon as the court dates ended the visits started faltering it was either 'exams' or 'friends' parties' or some other unmissable social event which stopped them from seeing her.

Molly was soon back in the courts again this time with expensive lawyers and she appealed for a psychological evaluation of the whole family to see what was wrong and why did the children not want to see her. This would need special permission and Molly was ready to bear all expenses.

The court agreed to restart the visits after this but these would need to be supervised initially.

Molly was seeing her own children being supervised like a criminal or a paedophile or a crook of some kind; this made her feel horrible but of course she would do anything just to see her children.

The supervised visits had to be done in various centres all around the city and she was given a date and a time for each. Molly brought in food and magazines for the children, she felt excited that she could see her children again, the social worker helped them to start talking, her son would bring a game with him and continue playing, her daughter was there too, still very angry.

After the second visit, the social worker suggested not to include her daughter in the visits because she was obstructing the relationship between Molly and her son.

Molly and her son always had a superb time, he wanted a dog so they went and booked a puppy together. It was so exciting and happy. Molly began to feel normal again.

The courts assessed the situation and removed all objections to the visiting. He could now stay any hours anytime go on holiday stay the weekend, anything.

They used to meet up every Saturday, go for a film and then eat out or sometimes he would come to Molly's, he got very friendly with her husband and they would cook and eat together, discuss books and movies and politics.

But as they came closer, Molly could see the blocks, her son would not stay more than three hours, four at the most, her ex was always texting him when he was with Molly. Molly had a room all set up in her hew house for her son. She ordered a bespoke computer desk and cupboards so he could stay over, do his homework, play on his computer, etc.

This was done by a top company as Molly wanted nothing but the best for her little prince. But this never happened and Molly felt really sad and lonely.

It was really lovely when he was there with Molly and she could see that her son really cared for her but then gradually the exams and friend's birthdays and other parties were happening more frequently than ever. This was very difficult for Molly because she did not have any more money to go to the lawyers.

Imagine her happiness when she got an email saying that her children wanted to see her.

Molly was very hopeful that things were taking a turn for the better. She planned to cook their favourites and bought some magazines for her daughter which she used to like and off she went full of love and hope, to meet them. She had no idea what was about to happen and maybe it's a good thing she did not.

Chapter 16

Molly's favourite niece is getting married back home, the wedding has been planned for months now and Molly has been looking forward to it as one looks forward to the last wedding in a whole generation.

With it being planned in January, Molly's usual annual visit to see her parents and cousins, the timing was nothing less than propitious and Molly was determined to make full use of it.

Enter Covid and all the big plans were halted, the wedding went ahead as planned with very few invitees as the families had been waiting some time and Molly had to make do with looking at pics on Facebook or listening to the cousins who had been to the party.

It was dismal to say the least and anyone who lives 5,000 miles from their family will understand what this is about. It is about meeting everyone, the comfort and warmth of your own family, the endless partying that is part of every wedding and the lovely saris and food.

It's often difficult to console oneself so Molly tried to throw herself headlong into work and keep herself busy that way. She loved doing different things at work, she was setting up family planning clinics and this took up nearly all her spare time.

Molly worked in a deprived part of the city where the women were not educated or independent. They were used by the men, the very same people who were supposed to love and protect them, for childbearing and housekeeping among other things and often against their will.

Molly decided that contraception will give these patients some say in their own lives and time to train, to learn English and to become less dependent. The response was initially lukewarm as they had just come out of Covid and maybe patients did not know what to expect but now it's very successful. Molly runs these clinics every six weeks with an experienced nurse fitting contraceptive devices. She just finished a long day last week, of fifteen patients and already there is a waiting list building up to the next one. It is heartening to see women making decisions about when to start, when to pause and when to consider their family complete. She speaks to all of them before the clinic day to make sure they are not pressurised into making any decisions and that they are aware of the pros and cons of the process.

Its hard work, no denying that, but intensely satisfying. She loves to see the women smile when they leave the clinic, thanking her and the team.

After the long day last week, Molly thought she would celebrate by going on a long drive.

It was lovely despite the fact that the sat nav crashed and she and her pup landed in a tiny village miles away from where they were planning to go. Mol just parked the car, they got out, walked in the sun, bought piping hot fish and chips from the village store and ate it in one of the pub garden style benches while her puppy sniffed at the chips, not sure whether to bite into one.

The weather held and it did not cloud over or rain even once while they were out, so a really nice day out, considering.

While driving back, with her tummy full of fish and chips with hot gravy and luminous green mushy peas and the car on the motorway cruising comfortably at 80 mph, Mol's thoughts wandered.

Her mind drifted back to when she was always the passenger, never the driver, in a long drive, because Molloy could not take the tension of her driving and after trying a few times, Mol thought that if she was driving to give him a break, it was having the opposite effect, he was so tense while she drove that she stopped driving completely when he was present. This went down very well with him, it was all about control, of course. Now with the benefit of hindsight it is clear as day but then it was all muddled and confusing.

People around her said he cared for her that was why he would not let her drive. He would not let her touch his car to even practice changing gears when Molly was learning to drive. This was what her instructor had suggested but after asking Molloy once, she decided not to ask him ever again.

Imagine Molly's surprise when a few years later, when she was working in a hospital about three hours from home, Molloy saying he had just bought a new car to come and see her over the weekend.

"A new car? But why a new car? You already have a car." It all came out then that Molloy's friend's wife was driving Molloy's car and she had crashed the car so badly that it was written off. Hence the hasty, "I have bought a new car to come and see you over the weekend" scenario. Molly was amazed, so the same rules did not apply to everyone, friends' wives were different and enjoyed privileges she never had.

She was taking lessons then on an old banger they had bought for less than five hundred pounds. Molly loved driving and even though she had not qualified in the UK, she used her Indian licence to go off on her own on weekend mornings.

She was working near Gateshead in the north east then. There was no sat nav and it was not possible for Molly to look at a map and drive when she was a beginner herself, so she just drove straight on for as long as she could and then came back. She still remembers the signs saying South Tyneside/Gateshead centre. She understood that to be able to drive, one has to drive alone, that's the only way to build confidence.

She remembered her in-laws clearly and their complicated dynamics with their son and her parents.

It was a nightmare.

She tried her very best to look after them only to be met with the severe criticism and hurtful comments about her upbringing. It was soul destroying to be so unloved.

Listening to one of her school mates about how her marriage had been completely arranged by her parents and how she had barely met her husband before the big day, Mol wondered if she could have done that. Maybe she could have, if she hadn't fallen head over heels for Molloy when she was 18.

The words young and foolish spring to mind, don't they? He was 23, a newly qualified intern and had just broken up with his girlfriend of six years which is a very long time when you are barely 18. They finally got married after Molly's graduation when she was 23 years old. The six years of courtship were heavenly, things could not have been rosier and she could tell her parents and her brother who had initially opposed the idea: "See, we are very happy, I told you, didn't I."

But time has a way of bringing people together and then pushing them apart so they had come together like lightning and now after a few years in England, they drifted apart slowly and steadily like clouds on a sunny day.

Was Molly in denial or could she genuinely not see what was happening? It was hard to say which was true but she believed her marriage was indestructible and that divorce and separation and infidelity happened to 'other people in soppy sentimental films'.

Is that why it happened? Maybe so. If she knew her marriage needed saving, she would have tried to do something about it.

Some of her friends had suggested, why don't you stay next to him all the time? Stay right next to him then he won't be able to mess about. They meant well and were trying to help but Molly thought, *what kind of love needs guarding? That is not love that is property.*

My husband is my love and if he needs guarding then there is no love there. Instead, she kept working longer hours, looking after Molloy's friends and their families over the weekend, and trying drink herself to oblivion when she could not sleep.

Funnily enough, all of Molloy's friends who she had wined and dined in her house never sparing any expense or any effort after working the whole week herself, promptly unfriended her after the divorce. They refused to even say hello if they bumped into each other in a gathering, and these were the very people Molly had thought of as family. She felt betrayed and isolated and struggled very hard to cope with the fact that they were not friends anymore. It still hurts to think about them and how they changed.

By this time, her ex had already moved to a different room, would not appear in any pictures with her and when she wanted to say married to him on her profile in Facebook, he would not allow it. Mol did not ask or speak to anyone but thought this was very unusual.

She was becoming very depressed and suffered from explosive headaches all day, she literally lived on paracetamol and brought packets of the stuff nearly every day. Molloy was totally unfazed, he carried on doing his music shows, functions, singing with his friend's wife and rehearsing with her for hours/days.

These functions were usually on a Saturday night so he would go to hers, stay overnight on Friday, then do the function on Saturday, stay over the weekend, go to work from hers on Monday and come home after work on Monday.

Molly was left to herself over the weekend, managing the house and two young kids on her own, she missed Molloy's company but realised that he loved music and understood he needed it for his happiness.

She did not confide in girlfriends because she felt she should not be talking about Molloy behind his back.

She was astronomically stupid but did speak to her own doctor who organised some therapy sessions for depression and anxiety. Molly still remembers the therapist, she was very good and after listening to her story, she said, "You are an intelligent woman; you know what to do."

Mol knew what she meant, but she could not do that, the kids were young, they needed both parents and both sets of grandparents would be very shocked.

She took it upon herself to persevere but she had overestimated herself. There was one birthday party that she remembers specifically where she was standing facing her ex and could see him making eyes at one of his friends' wife across the room.

They were all married to rich and busy husbands, had grown up kids and were bored to death. So, when he gave them attention, they eagerly lapped it up and begged for more. They said give me more and he gave generously, he was forever speaking or texting them. He had personal passwords to everything—his phone, his email, his account, it was all very private.

Lots of married couples she knew shared an email address, she could never imagine that with Molloy.

Oddly enough, he was transparent about finances, he shared a bank account with Mol and their salaries went into one account.

He helped a lot of his extended family as they were not well off including poor students in India. He had Molly's full support in all of this. They had a folder of brilliant but very poor students who had all scored highly in their board exams but were unable to continue studying due to financial pressures. They went to Kolkata armed with the folder and met each one of these students.

The students were all very polite and came with their teacher or their dad. Molly had cooked brunch but most of them declined, they all lived outside the city and had travelled in by train or bus to meet them. Molly thought maybe they were too embarrassed to eat, she did not press any further.

They had to bring their mark sheet with them and after checking their marks, Molly and Molloy would discuss how much the boy/girl needed on a monthly basis for his/her education and they would organise the money then.

Molly and Molloy supported a folder full of needy students paying for their education and also often their housing and medical needs till they were old enough to start working.

They handed out many thousands of rupees to these students over the years and Molly felt this was one of their good deeds.

She admired him for these charitable acts and always gave him her fullest support. Mol remembers her MIL was unhappy that they were doling out huge sums of money to poor students but Molly was happy they were helping the less fortunate. All their friends were saving for their next property or their next holiday or both, only very few friends came forward to help them.

Mol was not sure whether she should write about all this, would anyone be interested? There was only one way to find out—write.

And if she did not tell the story of her life, who will?

Chapter 17

A Child.

"Holding my little boy's hand on the way to school is such a fantastic feeling; this must be what touching god feels like because I firmly believe that little children have a piece of heaven in them."

A child is like a river, flowing naturally and beautifully.

There is no reason to not like a river in all its spontaneous beauty. But think about it, when the same river is harnessed into a hydropower project, it irrigates fields and meadows and feeds millions of hungry children every day.

So should we try and make every river into a hydropower project or should we let all rivers be as they were and let the children starve instead?

The answer, of course, is neither, it lies somewhere in between. I hate parents who terrorise their children with corporal punishment or threats into doing what they think is right for the child, who think that scoring the highest mark in every exam is going to win them the Oscars for parenthood.

I detest them and nothing could be far from what I think is right. However, I understand a little bit of where these parents are coming from, especially in all developing countries without any government support or benefits for citizens without work etc.

You might have great respect for your fellow humans, listen to everything your seniors say, treat women with dignity but sadly that does not guarantee a job, a roof over your head, two square meals a day, medical fees when you are ill.

Over and above everything I want for my child, I want him to be alive and healthy and what better way to ensure a healthy future than to make sure he will be able to secure his own career, I ask you.

I am a believer in hard graft and training. 99% perspiration, 1% inspiration, etc.

As parents, we have to inspire our children to work towards a goal, we have to motivate them to focus on what they wish to become, not what we want them to be.

"Our children come through us and not from us"—Kahlil Gibran. We are merely the caretakers of these young people with great potential and it rests on us to help them realise their true worth and blossom into mature human beings.

Chapter 18

Molly arrived as planned.

When she got the email, she suggested that both Molloy and his wife and Molly and the children could meet up but Molloy suggested this meeting would be 'stressful' and that it should just be Molly and her children. Molly agreed, decades of habit of agreeing to anything Molloy said.

Not that she was in their lives in any shape or form except in the form of letters and emails and texts and phone calls that went unanswered.

So why did they wish to inflict all this pain?

Because they wanted to tell her what a horrid, miserable, unkind, fake, lying, unstable person she was and how difficult it was to keep in touch with her because of her aforementioned qualities. They did not feel safe with her, she ran away with money from the house after the divorce, she never looked after them even before the divorce. She was the bad guy and it was all because of her. It was Her Fault.

Her daughter had written all this out and was speaking with such a sharpness that Molly felt the words slicing through her heart, she tried to remember the little girl who loved to dress up, the little girl whom she loved more than life itself, the little girl for whom she bought expensive French dresses when all she could afford for herself was second-hand clothes from a charity shop. The little girl who loved makeup and jewellery and going out, just like Molly.

Her son was biologically sixteen but psychologically much younger as boys tend to be; he was following and copying everything his sister said or did. So after her daughter finished telling her about her past life for about an hour, he followed with his own statement for about a quarter of an hour, his style of talking was casual, less sharp but very sarcastic.

Again, Molly was the reason everything had gone wrong, she was the One Person responsible for everything bad.

She had taken the favourite things for each of her children, magazines/soft roulette cheese/spag Bol/Guylaine egg for her daughter and Chinese noodles and marvel egg for her son.

She had also bought matching containers for them careful not to take big amounts as that had put them off in the past, so two round boxes with soft clasps round the edges matching in size and design she was so happy she had found them, they were just right. She imagined them grabbing a fork and eating out of the little round boxes, the stupid dreamer that she was. As Molly walked in to what used to be her house, she was struck by how much stuff there was, and how glamorous and opulent everything was, the kitchen was full of the latest appliances and looked like a showroom, wow.

Before sitting down on the white chair, she took everything out of the bag and placed it on the table, both the children glanced but did not say anything, no thank you, none at all, just cold stares. "I have cooked for you guys," Molly said and her daughter said she had just had a roast lunch and could not eat anything.

She sounded friendly when she said she had now moved out, still did not drive and she offered Molly a cup of tea. Molly was feeling hopeful at this point, maybe they will see me regularly again.

But what followed was not a discussion but a tirade of accusations and Molly sat there in stunned silence and forgot to speak, mainly because she was crying.

The children took turns in hitting out at her and they—her own flesh and blood—knew exactly what would hurt, and they had prepared well. Molly's daughter read out a piece she had written on her phone and her son just spoke, both devastating.

After they had finished speaking and her daughter had mentioned in passing that she just offered her tea because she was polite, Molly did not want the tea anymore.

Molloy and his present wife were upstairs and Molly was sure they could hear every word. Such clever people, to not be present for the record but to listen in on everything, that's the way to do it.

She was given time to speak but she could not speak much, because she was crying so hard it was difficult to do both. She said she was sorry that she wished them well and will always be there for them, said her goodbyes and left.

To this day, Molly is not sure how she drove back after this, she was crying so hard she could hardly see where she was going. She had rung her brother because she knew she could not ring her mother.

Her friends felt she had gone very quiet all of a sudden. They planned to come and see her. It was great to see her friends and for a few hours Molly would become her old bubbly witty self.

The days were long and the nights longer.

Molly helped herself by taking long walks, speaking to her parents and started meditating.

She did not stop working, but it was a struggle to stay normal, every single word the children had said hurt her like a knife in her stomach and each time she thought it hurt more instead of less.

What was that about time being a great healer? If ever there was such a thing.

Chapter 19

Today, watching young children playing together while waiting in line at the airport reminded Molly of her and her cousins when they were in school. She was the oldest among her cousins and though they were all boys, she was the tallest and strongest then. That is really funny because now they are all much taller and stronger than her. They would meet every Sunday for the whole day and Molly has fond memories of these Sundays. They would play family-family or play Germans and Americans, the second one was Molly's favourite.

They would set up trenches under her grandma's bed and open fire on the enemy who were under another bed. The beds used to be very big and high then so Molly and her cousins could sit up straight under them while planning to attack the 'enemy'.

Sometimes one group would go on a march and then come under sniper attack from the enemy group—it was good fun. The other interesting fact was that there was a lot of food stored under the beds in those days (refrigerators were a rarity) under heavy metallic net covers that the cat/wind could not knock over. So they could sneak in a tasty snack while playing under the bed that was a real plus.

Molly being the oldest and strongest then helped her cousins lift the metal covers, prise open steel tiffin boxes that they were not strong enough to do then. The only time that she protested was when her cousins started chomping on a pile of fried fish stored under the bed and she was worried they might have fish bones stuck in their throat.

She tried to stop them but the excitement of doing something they were not supposed to do was so great that they did not listen and kept pushing more fish into their mouths.

Luckily, one of Molly's aunts came in to the room at this point and stopped them. Molly being the only girl in the group was always given extra special treatment. When she grew up and heard about how girls in other families come second to the boys, she felt very guilty and lucky at the same time.

She always had priority over her brothers as a child and strangely enough still did in her own side of the extended family. She joked about this saying she used to be a VIP before marriage and after marriage she became an asylum seeker. That is probably how a lot of girls feel but Molly being herself could laugh and talk about it openly with her friends.

On those Sundays, the whole family would go for films, usually Bruce Lee or Charlie Chaplin that was newly released. They would also watch classics like the *Guns of Navarone, Where Eagles Dare*, easily taking up a whole row of seats.

There would be so much food, each of the uncles would treat them. There would be hand-cut crisps, ice-cream and of course popcorn with spicy samosas/prawn cutlets for the grown-ups.

Molly feels she lives on a different planet now, watching films by herself with a small pack of popcorn.

After a while, she stopped buying popcorn as she could not finish even the smallest box. She tried to ask her friends to come but they were married with kids and when she came home from work and was free to call them, they were at their busiest with kids and family.

The other problem was that Molly, being brought up on a certain genre of films, could not watch the girlie films that most other women liked. This made it very hard for her to find company and she got used to idea of watching films alone. These were two things she could not imagine, watching films alone and eating alone in a restaurant. She has not done the second but she has been to umpteenth concerts and films by herself. The first time she went up to the counter and bought a single ticket, the man at the counter asked her twice—single ticket? You mean, just one ticket? She felt like saying can you not see there is just me? Are you blind?

Like many other things, it did not affect her anymore. Or so she liked to think.

Chapter 20

Molly was running late, work started at nine, it was already half-past eight and she was still not in her car. It had been very hot the last two days and both Molly and her pooch struggled to sleep.

Running to the car with her work bag and flask of coffee, Molly opened the car door and was back home in a split second, the door handle nearly burnt her hand and the car was full of sweet warm air that rushed out as she opened the door. "You are going to be late for school and baba will be late, for work," Molly could hear her mum's voice clearly as she scrambled into their Maruti Omni, dragging the heavy school bag after her.

The door handle nearly burnt her hand and the car had a sweet warm air in it as she struggled to roll down the window. Baba was starting the car now and would soon drop her off in school and she would be joining the school assembly.

Molly quickly prayed, "Please God, I don't want to be in the latecomer's line," knowing fully well that that was very likely to happen.

On other, more normal days, Molly's close friend came over and hurried her along, they would both walk to the bus stop and take a bus to school. It was against the general traffic such that both going and coming from school they got nearly empty buses. None of the shouty pushy over-crowded ones, thank God.

Back when they lived in the north east frontier area, Molly used to go to the missionary school in a medium-sized van, the winding mountain roads were not wide enough for a small bus let alone the usual mega school buses we see in cities.

The missionary school had been built initially for the children of the indigenous people of the area but later government servants had made a petition to allow their children to study there. This was granted but civilian children could only attend as day scholars whereas the other kids were boarders there. The military children had their own school though some preferred to go to the missionary school as it was very well thought of at the time.

So the modest little school van would pick up Molly and her brother at 8.30 every morning and drop them back at 4.30 in the afternoon.

Once the van had some engine problem, so that day they went to school in a dark green military truck, Molly remembers they had to climb into the back and there were sacks of pineapples and they had to sit carefully as the gunny bags were itchy and the pineapples prickly.

It was open and felt strange. There was a very wobbly bridge on the river Siang, later known as the Brahmaputra in the wide plains of Assam and Molly remembers the bridge swayed even more when the truck went on it that day.

You could see the river at the deep end of the gorge, rushing and frothing over the sharp rocks and here they were, casually driving across it on a loose bridge.

Molly found later that the bridge was loose for a reason, it was an army bridge and could be taken apart in a few hours in case of war/invasion; the Chinese border was not far.

It's amazing how well adjusted the locals were, you could see them sitting on the bridge, legs dangling over on the side, trying to catch fish from the gorge, looking at them from the van scared Molly then.

While all of this was going on with Molly, her brother, only eighteen months younger, was completely fearless and lived in a different world. He had thrown himself into a mountain stream for fun, luckily Molly dragged him out on time, he had tried eating wild herbs that the indigenous children foraged and ate, he had tried to run away from class with a fellow adventurer and attempted to walk home but again someone had seen them and contacted the school. So yes Molly's brother was the complete opposite.

He just experimented with himself (jumping into the stream) with instruments(he would flick a lighter under a mercury thermometer to see how fast the mercury would shoot, this meant there were never any working thermometers in the house) and he loved taking apart things like torches, wristwatches, ball point pens because he wanted to know how they worked.

The main problem was that after he had taken them apart, he could not put them back together and admitting to any of this he risked a serious hiding, so he promptly got rid of the evidence.

So all of Molly's childhood, she would see family members searching for that new ballpoint pen or that shiny new torch someone bought last week, knowing fully well they were never going to find anything at all. Molly was not fearless or adventurous not by a long shot but she was happy to go along with her brother when they would both sneakily drink condensed milk from the tin. This could only be done when Mum was in the shower so needed proper organisation and meticulous planning. And yes, they pulled it off most days except that Mum could take one look at the tin and understand why it was so quiet when she was in the shower but she preferred not to mention it.

Some years later, when her brother was a young boy, he began to spend hours in the toilet and after a lot of questioning it came out that he was standing on two large pieces of soap and skating across the floor of the bathroom. No one not even Molly's mum knew quite how to react to this. He always used his legs to switch the lights or fans off or on, these being the old style toggle switches, his flexibility was amazing. Visitors to the house would stare open-mouthed, Molly was sure they had never seen anyone operate switches with their feet and of course Molly herself had never seen anyone else do the same ever. It was funny and embarrassing and exasperating all at the same time.

Her brother Sam was a natural leader and he was always the leader of the group. Whenever they went to a new town and with Molly's dad's job, they moved every eighteen months to two years, Molly's brother made friends with the whole neighbourhood in one week flat.

He changed completely when he hit teenage, he stayed in and read and read, and would only catch up with a select group of friends once a month. He started playing the violin and with sheer hard work topped his class and his music exams. Molly's dad played the violin too and there came a time when you could not tell whether it was her dad or her brother playing and this within less than three years of starting to play.

Once there was a competition in school, a wildlife quiz and the three top students could go on a free trip to the sunder bans, the famous mangrove forests to the south of Bengal, the home of the famous Royal Bengal tiger. Molly remembers he brought the whole set of wildlife encyclopaedias to his own room from the living room bookcase and read them cover to cover. It was no surprise when he was chosen for the free school trip next week.

Molly was so proud of him.

They now live many thousands of miles apart and Molly misses him every day, it's so unfair, we used to live in the same house now we don't even live in the same country and only manage to meet up once a year if we are lucky.

Molly remembers the first house they lived in in north eastern India. It was on the top of a small hill and you had to go up a lot of steps to enter the compound. The house was brand new, a bungalow with a green lawn ran all round it and it had banana trees at the back like all other houses in the area. Molly and Sam used to love the little cement canals all around the house. These were built as drains but were never used. Molly and Sam pretended these were rivers and built bridges on them, it was great fun, Sam was the engineer and Molly his erstwhile assistant.

On the left side of the front lawn, there was a little square cemented area, this was where they mixed the cement when they built the house, and after a spell of rain this area caught a bit of the water and attracted loads of birds who flew in to have a bath.

Molly remembers hiding behind a curtain while she watched all the birds coming to have a bath, sashay in the water, throwing little sprays of water around and then taste the fruit of the guava tree in the corner of the garden. The guavas were soft and sweet with a bright red centre and the birds loved eating them.

They also had quite a few chickens in the back, they lived in a big hen house and laid fresh eggs every day. During their stay there was some talk of a disease in the chicken so each chicken had to swallow a single clove of garlic for prevention. Before the chicken coop was built, something strange happened, their hen called Kali who was matronly and sweet with salt and pepper feathers suddenly started to disappear during the day. She would only come into the kitchen at night where Molly's mum left a plate of rice for her. So Kali was nowhere all day, she appeared at night, finished the plate of rice in five seconds and disappeared again.

This went for quite a while and no one had a clue.

Molly still remembers it was early on a Sunday morning when they heard noises coming from the ceiling, it was a bungalow, so that was strange all right.

Suddenly they could hear Kali cackling from the roof and Molly and Sam ran out to see what Kali was doing on the roof.

What they saw was unforgettable, Kali had laid eggs on the roof, these had hatched and now the new-born chicks were trying to fly down from the roof to the garden.

Molly and Sam ran into the house and ran out with a large bedcover, they held it stretched out under the roof so the chicks could jump from the roof onto the cover and land safely.

Now Molly knew why Kali was behaving so strangely.

By early afternoon, the commotion had settled and it was lovely seeing Kali the proud mother hen walking around the back yard cackling happily and swinging her bottom in the air while the chicks followed her in a row. Molly would make a paste of flour and chicken feed to feed them twice daily.

The little chicks were always hungry and they grew fast. Molly and Sam soon had a flock of chickens and that's when the hen house was built for them.

It was a large wooden house with lots and lots of wooden poles running the whole length. Molly went in to explore and was surprised at how big and airy it was inside. There were a few chickens roosting on the poles while others were outside picking food.

During weekends and school holidays, Molly spent a long time playing and feeding the chickens—she can still clearly see the bungalow they lived in with the backyard framed by the banana trees and the big hen house. The bungalow was on the top of a small hill and the little town they lived in was nestled in a valley, surrounded by high mountains.

In winter, Molly could wake up and see the snow shining on the mountains all around, it was spectacular. Sometimes at night the military cantonment would throw a party and they would make lamps out of old tins of condensed milk and put them all round the fence. From the valley where Molly lived, these lamps looked like rings of light gleaming in the darkness, like stars on the ground.

Like all good things, their stay came to an end when Molly's dad was transferred to his next posting. Kali was expecting again and Molly was worried how she was going to cope with the move.

This was going to be a long drive down windy mountain roads and then a long distance again once they reached the plains. After a lot of discussion, Molly's parents decided that Kali would travel in comfort in a large wicker basket lined with straw and old newspapers. This basket was carefully placed in the boot of the car with heavy boxes all around it so that if the road was bumpy, the boxes would take the main brunt of it.

Each time they stopped for fuel or tea or for anything, they would open the boot and check on Kali. She was sitting on her eggs when they had started, all her feathers puffed out, concentrating hard.

The second time they stopped, the first chick had hatched, and after that each time they stopped, Molly and Sam ran out of the car to see what was happening in the boot.

By the time they reached their new house, Kali had a whole new brood of baby chicks, all born in a wicker basket in the back of an ambassador, that was travelling from the winding mountain roads of Arunachal to the fertile plains of Assam.

Kali is an amazing and adventurous mum. *Imagine if we asked a human being to do the same,* thought Molly.

Chapter 21

Molly has been in England for many years now of which the major time was spent in and around London. She somehow always knew she would love London and she fell in love with London immediately.

By the time she had done her post-grad exams, Molly knew that she really could not live elsewhere. London truly had her in her embrace. She complained about the rain, the tube strikes, the crowds and all the other things we all complain about but the truth was she could not imagine living anywhere else in England.

She did meet a lot of patients from Europe as a lot of people moved from Europe to the UK after Brexit. She spoke to patients from Italy, Spain, France, Poland, Germany etc. and sometimes wondered what it would be like to settle in Europe—still very tempting but she would have to learn the local language first.

Back in India, Molly's childhood was spent in many different cities over the northern and eastern part of the country, as her dad had a transferable job. So she was quite used to the idea of moving right from her childhood. Molly firmly believed that travelling and living in different places is real education. But there's no denying it is hard work, harder as you get older and harder here because help is so expensive. Sometimes after the practice meeting on a Wednesday afternoon, the nurses would start talking about where they were born, which school they went to, and who with and Molly felt really homesick. She wished she could say things like—my brother has BT broadband, he said it's very good or my mum always buys fruit from Tesco. She has never had family here and she felt jealous when her colleagues talked about their families, their schoolmates all living in the same city.

If only I were so lucky, thought Molly. But the funny thing was, total strangers helped Molly all the time. Molly has often thought about this, do I look vulnerable? Why do people help me all the time?

She would be driving into a large car park when at least two cars would stop and give her their tickets as they were leaving anyway and there was paid time on the ticket that she could use. This has happened so often that it was an almost certainty.

She tries her best to keep small change for parking and was very nearly caught out when she parked near one of the farmers markets and the machine would only accept cash. She scrounged inside her bag, in the car and found a few coins but not enough. She then asked for help from a complete stranger who had just parked their car, paid parking and was going to the car to put the sticker on the windscreen. Molly explained that she needed a few more coins and that she would pay him back online, the gentleman straightaway gave her a fistful of change, more than what Molly needed and did not want to share bank details. Molly thanked him profusely, picked out what she needed and returned the rest of the change. *Such a generous man,* she thought.

The other day Molly was buying a few things at a superstore, it was the last week of the month and she was skint. She asked the lady at the till if they have a reduced to clear section, she said only the big stores have it all the time.

When it was Molly's turn to pay, the lady at the till asked her if she had a store card. Molly replied that she did not. At this point, the lady asked the customer behind her, he too did not have a store card. By this time, Molly was feeling embarrassed but the lady serving her was not giving up. She left the till and found someone in the staffroom with a store card, took their permission and did Molly's bill on the card, all to help Molly pay less for her shopping.

Molly was so touched tears came to her eyes, she thanked the lady effusively and quickly left the store, pretending to wipe her glasses.

There are still so many good people in the world.

Chapter 22

Molly missed her parents, and even though they had always been a very close-knit family, she now felt closer to her parents and missed them more. The fact that they were getting older and were so many thousand miles away did little to help, of course.

Molly hated the fact that her parents were getting older, each time she saw them she realised they were slowing down a little more.

She remembers her school days clearly, baba would come home from work and ask her and her brother if they had finished their homework. The moment they said yes, he would take them out, usually to a good film followed by dinner at a restaurant. Ma would try and protest saying dinner was ready but baba would say put it in the fridge, we will eat it tomorrow and off they went.

Molly remembers, Disney's *Jungle Book* was released on a Friday and of course, they saw it the first day it was released. There was some kind of a strike that started on the Saturday so Molly's friends and cousins could not watch because by the time the strike had ended, they had changed the film. It did not matter whether it was hot, cold, wet or thundery, Molly's dad still has total disregard of the surroundings if he wants to watch a film, like going for the new Bond film in the middle of Covid. It was very safe because they were the only people in the hall that evening.

The other fantastic thing was long drives. On weekends, they would wake up early and go on long drives in the country, stopping for tea and biscuits in a tiny tea stall by the road side. On these early morning drives, the roads would be deserted and Dad would take his hands off the wheel and show Molly—look the car is driving itself, it's a magic car—and Molly loved it. She still yearns for her childhood her beautiful young parents, her mischievous brother and the finicky sky blue ambassador with the flat red seats.

Her parents never pressured her to come first in class, they were happy as long as she stayed among the top five. Many of Molly's friends were under tremendous pressure at that point and she felt happy and relaxed that her parents were really chilled and modern.

Molly had both sets of grandparents and they got along like a house on fire, the two granddads would do the daily shop while the two grand moms were busy planning the menu for the day, with Molly's mum helping. It was a very happy and carefree childhood and this probably left Molly totally unprepared for adult life, she was not able to adjust with her in laws. She found them orthodox and narrow. They were well-off but had a very controlled lifestyle.

Molly struggled to fit in with them and their thoughts.

They did not like her and put everything down to her affluent lifestyle in the city which to be honest was just a normal middle-class lifestyle and not at all affluent, suppose it's a relative term anyway.

Love is not something that needs to be declared or spelt out, when you love someone they know it they feel it and when you don't love someone they get it too.

Molly felt unloved and unwelcome and felt that she was an appendage, not a family member. She was constantly told how hard the other young wives worked and how well they looked after their in-laws. But this just told her she was being compared with others, she was not valued for who she was, others she did not know and it felt very unfair.

The jewellery from her parents was a constant source of friction in the household, where should they keep it, how should they store it etc. kept getting discussed all the time and every time they sat down. This went on until she had to say, "It's my jewellery so I will look after it, please do not worry." Molly knew she was definitely in the bad books of her in-laws, but she did not believe in trying to become someone else to get into their good books. It does not seem such a bad idea now but at the age of twenty-three it was a no-no.

They did not want Molly to visit her parents but Molly missed her parents and her cousins and would try and visit them whenever she could. Molly kept in touch with her in laws because she did not want Molloy to miss his parents, they kept visiting Molly and Molloy every summer until her father in law passed and then her mum in law did not wish to travel anymore.

Molly looked after them as well as she could, took them out after she had learnt to drive and took them shopping, but they never bonded. It was always a polite and formal relationship and they would only ever confide in their son. Molly just happened to be someone their son had married against their wishes and that was that.

Chapter 23

"Hi Mols."

"Hi James, why are you calling me Mols?"

"Why don't you call me Jimjams?"

"I would rather call you Jammy Dodgers."

"You think I am dodgy, ha ha."

"Because they are my favourite biscuits, that's why."

"Where's Molloy?"

"He should be here, it must be the traffic, always worse this time of year."

"I spoke to the traffic warden and asked him to put on speed limits just so I can be with you, Mols"

"Very funny, very very funny I say."

"It's a joke, Mols, you don't have to react like that."

"Okay, I will go and check the oven…"

James, Jimjams, Jammy Dodgers was Molloy's work colleague but his friendly stubbornness or stubborn friendliness soon endeared him to Molly too.

She began to look at him as someone she could ring when Molloy was in a meeting and ask him to pick up their daughter from music lesson or someone to whom you could say, 'hey, can you pick up some milk and bread on your way here?'

They did have a lot of friends back then but somehow James was close to both Molly and Molloy.

So imagine Molly's surprise when James asks her to meet him for coffee at lunchtime. Molly was worried about James's mum as she had recently had her hip done and then developed an infection after the operation. This meant she could not go home, start physiotherapy, etc., and the delay in recovery was affecting her mentally and physically.

Molly helped as much as possible by speaking to Agnes, James's mum, liaising with the physio and the district nurses and talking to her GP to discuss management.

So when James sent her a message, Molly was sure Agnes had taken a bad turn and James needed her clinical advice.

"Hi James, how's Agnes?"

"Mum? She is dangerously well, and getting better every day, the physio is a genius, I tell you and the district nurses, they are angels in uniform."

"Hoh, I thought this was about Agnes."

"Hence the worried long face with the frown, I see."

"Of course, I am worried; it's only natural."

"Well, she is fine, you can stop worrying now."

"Yes master, I will switch it off right now."

"You look devastatingly sexy when you are angry, Mols."

"Stop it, James, I have come out of work thinking it's about Agnes, I have a visit after this."

"Well, let's not waste this coffee, won't take more than three minutes of your precious time."

"I am going; I have had enough."

"No, you are not, Mols, you are not."

James suddenly reached out and kissed her on the lips and to her utter surprise, she found herself kissing him back.

What was that all about?

What started with a kiss, grew like a cancer spreading slowly when no one was watching, and before long, James and Molly were in it.

Molly hated herself and would lie awake night after night thinking, *why why why. How can I do this to Molloy? He is so good to me and the kids, not knowing then that Molloy had carefully cultivated quite a harem behind her back.*

Looking back now with the advantage of hindsight, she feels maybe, just maybe, James knew what was going on and felt sorry for her. Maybe what he felt for her was sympathy, mistaken as love. Molly has been in love only with Molloy, she has not felt like that with anyone ever, she was not sure if she would feel that way with George Clooney or Brad Pitt. Jokes apart, the first cut is always the deepest, as they say.

With Jammy Dodgers, she felt he was a good friend and that was that. So when matters were semi-serious, she spoke to James and said she wanted to end it.

"I cannot do this, Jams, I cannot live with myself."

"What's wrong with love? You know how much I love you, Mols."

"That's not right for both of us please please, James, you know that."

"How do you know Molloy is not seeing someone else?"

"Are you crazy? How dare you say something like that? Do you have any proof of what you just said?"

"Calm down, Mols, it was only a comment."

"Really! Do not make such comments about my husband, I am warning you."

"Aww, come here baby, you look fantastic."

"No, no James, I do not want this, please stop seeing me."

"What? You don't want to see me? Seriously?"

"Yes, seriously. It is wrong James; I cannot do this."

"But how can love be wrong?"

"Please James, stop seeing me, I don't want to discuss anything, please."

Shortly after this, James received a job offer from Indonesia which he duly accepted. Molly was sad and happy, upset and pleased, it was a real rollercoaster of emotions. As the days went past, the weeks, months and years rolled by, Molly began to see what James had hinted at.

Molloy was intelligent and very private. He was on the phone, literally all the time. Molly's friends kept saying why don't you ask him, but Molly felt it was his business. She especially remembers the children's parents' evenings; Molloy would be on the phone the whole time. If anyone remarked about how busy he was on the phone, he would then say that he had to do everything for the house because Molly did not do the basics. He chipped away at her confidence and self-esteem for years and years.

Molly believed every word he uttered to the extent that when they divorced Molly was not sure she could look after the house and the kids. She had heard that she was forgetful, inefficient, she had no idea of finances and her driving skills were a joke constantly, in seriousness and in jest for the last three decades. So, she believed that she was all of those things. When they had a house extension, Molly asked for a few things and Molloy said no to all of them. Molly was hurt but her parents were shocked, how could he do this? Isn't this your house too?

Molly tried to calm them: it's okay, his ideas are probably better than mine. Molly now runs her house and she knows you do not have to be on the phone 24/7 to run a household. It's taken her a few years to find out that she is not what Molloy had said she was. She was a strong woman whose only mistake was loving and trusting someone who wanted to control her life. How to control someone who is confident? Easy, try to undermine their confidence and play on their weaknesses.

Molly felt then that Molloy was doing a very difficult job looking after the bills and the taxes etc. She felt inadequate and grateful towards Molloy for his help.

She was managing two kids, their homework, their school, their line of birthday parties, play dates and sleepovers, she was coping with full time work as a GP, entertaining Molloy's friends and managing everything with a smile.

She did not speak to anyone, not her girlfriends, who were Molloy's friends' wives who stopped talking to her as soon as they divorced, not James, she thought this was all private, she was magnificently stupid.

Hindsight, of course, is fabulous.

The other day, she was rushing to go on a visit, and as she rushed into the car with her work bag, she remembered having coffee with James as if it was yesterday.

Wonder where he was, must be out partying with his stunning Indonesian wife, Molly chuckled to herself.

God bless Jammy Dodgers.

Chapter 24

Molly's family is very musical; both her parents are amateur singers and they love taking part in cultural shows. After her dad's retirement, this has kept them busy, everyone including Molly was worried how he would cope because he was a well-known workaholic but his musical side came to his rescue and the family breathed a sigh of relief.

As a young girl, Molly secretly wanted to play the piano but what with one thing and another, it never happened. Imagine her surprise then when one of her retired friends offered her a piano. She was relocating to Aberdeen to spend time with her grandchildren and though the piano was old, it was still in tune.

Molly was beside herself with happiness, she thanked her friend profusely and started looking into lessons, etc. The piano would need tuning first of course.

She started taking online lessons as she found them convenient though no less expensive than face to face lessons. Learning to read music was like learning a language, Molly was really excited.

Molly's daughter used to play the piano really well, Molly used to drive her to her tutor's house twice a week and she soon realised her daughter was a natural musician.

The tutor was a girl in her twenties who had done up to grade eight in four different instruments, she also sang well and her dad was a semi-professional singer. She was small and chubby and a completely awesome pianist.

When in the tutor's house, Molly's daughter started both singing and playing the piano. Her tutor told Molly that she should encourage her daughter to pursue a career in music. Molly was overjoyed, yes, that will be fantastic. She could see her daughter in a lovely white gown playing a shiny black Steinway on stage and curtseying in response to a standing ovation from the audience, *Oooh,* thought Molly, *just fabulous.*

Her daughter would finish basic studies, then study music in a famous conservatoire, travel the world as a musician, she could have it all. But things did not go as expected, her daughter refused to work hard, she did not want to work hard and was as Molly found out soon, did not want to be a pianist. Even so, when she played, even the noisiest audience fell totally quiet, such was the magic in her music. Molly had begged and pleaded with her to practise for a friend's birthday party.

The same thing happened, the audience was as noisy as you would expect at a thirteenth birthday party but as soon as Molly's daughter started playing, everyone stopped and listened. It was a beautiful piece and the audience loved it. This was nearly two decades back but Molly remembers it like it was yesterday, she had anticipated that people will ask for another piece but try as she might, her daughter would not agree to practice a second piece.

So when people were praising her daughter and requesting an encore, she had to say that her daughter did not wish to play another. Molly is completely different, she is not one-tenth as musical as her daughter and though she has had some dance training that her mum wanted her to have, she had never had any piano lessons.

Sitting in front of the piano practising, her mind wandered to the piano tutor's house, all her certificates framed on the wall, how well her daughter sang and played then and she sat there longing for those times that will never come back.

Her daughter, beautiful and talented, could have done so much more with life. She was the apple of her daddy's eye, why did Molloy not encourage her then?

Molly does not know the answer but she knows she has tried her best. All she knows is that with just a little effort her daughter could have had a successful career, but…

Of course, when and if this ever came up, the whole blame is squarely on Molly's shoulders. She is the reason her daughter did not do as expected.

This had the desired effect, of course. It made Molly feel incompetent and her self-esteem was in her boots then. Unfortunately, she was never the reason why something went well, never.

Looking back, Molly felt she now had her own life to live and she was trying her best to make a semi success of what was left of it.

Molly sincerely hoped her daughter will return to music someday as that is where she belongs, though she does not know it yet.

Chapter 25

When she first landed in this country, her neighbours were surprised to find that Christmas was celebrated in India.

Molly's hometown was the capital of the British Raj for two hundred years so the Christmas tradition is very strong and strangely has very little to do with being Christian.

Christmas was the time for super sweet cakes, fake cigarettes made of sugar with a bit of red colouring on the tip to make it look real, Christmas trees of all shapes and sizes, little Santa Clauses made of snow white cotton wool and bright red cloth, miles of shiny red bunting and of course lots of partying.

At her first Christmas in this country, Molly made roast turkey, the traditional Christmas fare, but no one liked turkey and it became a struggle to finish.

After that first year, they usually have roast lamb or oak ham chicken. Molly loves everything about Christmas—the tree with lights, the stockings hanging by the fireplace, milk and cookies for Santa, presents for the children and of course a sumptuous Christmas dinner, usually lamb or chicken.

When she was married to Molloy, all their friends came with families and the house was full of children and toys and food. It was so magical. Molly remembers one year there were so many dinner guests that they ran out of chairs and had to make do with using side tables as chairs for the young kids.

Molly's Christmas special was roast lamb with rosemary and veggies with cheese followed by sticky toffee pudding. It was always a huge hit, especially the kids loved it and asked for seconds. Happy memories.

After her divorce, their friends became his friends overnight. To be totally honest, they were Molloy's friends to begin with but after many years of spending weekends and going on holidays and partying together, she thought of them as her friends too.

That was her stupidity and she got what she deserved.

The first Christmas after her divorce, one of her friends (her friend—she knew the difference now) asked her to come and stay over, knowing she had no one to celebrate with. Molly was very grateful and stayed with the family. They were warm and they pulled her into them with love and hugs.

None of her old friends, the people she loved and missed so much, even sent her a card or a text. It was as if her life with them never existed.

How can they cut me off just because we have divorced? Molly still wondered.

Her school friends tried telling her that they were never her friends; if they were, they would never leave her, especially in a crisis. They have a point. Molly knew they were probably right but she could not bring herself to admit that all the fun all the happiness and the laughter she enjoyed with them was fake, that it was not real friendship.

But coming from Kolkata, educated by Roman Catholics in a tiny convent that was notoriously difficult to get into, Molly still loves Christmas and when people complain, why we are selling Christmas tree and tinsel in September, she can see both sides of the argument.

She went shopping after work today and bought a little nativity set that caught her fancy. *Money was tight as always was but this set will be a Christmas present to me,* she thought. She still remembers going up to the school chapel in the mornings, how they had to touch the sponge containing water of the Jordan and genuflect before entering. The chapel was small in size but had strong and very peaceful vibes.

Molly remembers wanting to sit and enjoy the peace that one felt only in such beautiful places.

Molly felt she was religious by nature and felt attracted to places of worship especially churches from a young age. After studying in a convent from nursery to sixth form, she had asked her parents' permission to convert to Christianity and become a nun when she was about sixteen. Her parents were not surprised and her dad said—people who change religions have not understood the first thing, that all religions say the same thing.

Molly thought long and hard about this and decided not to, there was logic in what her dad said.

But then she knew churches were her weakness and never thought anything of it until she met a vicar quite by chance who was protesting against the huge effort and finances that went into the building and maintenance of large churches. This vicar said quite plainly, well we just need a place for people to gather, but the place is not more important than the people. Of course not, thought Molly wondering why she had never thought of it like this. It is true that the building of a church nearly always gets more attention than the congregation. Maybe all that attention is misplaced. She remembers a long conversation with the vicar who said that he worked from a normal house converted into a church and that suited everyone just fine.

Time for a rethink then, thought Molly. She was aware that all religions spend a large amount on the place of worship. What if those funds were diverted to mental health for young people, homeless charities and the like. The building has always had more attention than the people and it was now time to change that.

When the Notre Dame burnt down a few years back, record sums of money came in from all parts of the world. Sadly, no such thing happens when children go hungry or homeless people die of hypothermia in winter. It is shocking but we do like our buildings more than we like our fellow humans. Lesson learnt.

Chapter 26

It had rained all week and people thought, *Oh it has rained all week, it will stop over the weekend.* It promptly rained all weekend too. There was no dearth of rain clouds sailing up, hitting the Pennines and coming down as rain.

The rain fell in big drops on the ground, on the tee tops and on the top of Molly's conservatory, making a pleasant pitter patter.

"I hear leaves drinking rain, I hear rich leaves on top, giving the poor beneath, drop after drop. Tis a sweet noise to hear, these green leaves drinking near…"

The builder had suggested a different type of roof so that the rain would not make a noise but Molly said no, I don't mind the noise, please do not give me a special roof. She wanted to say I love the sound of rain but decided this was information her builder could do without, so she merely insisted that she does not need a special roof, just a usual one would do. Sitting with a coffee in her conservatory after a spell of rain when nature would be resting after a large drink, she would listen to slow soft classical piano. It was achingly beautiful; the rain and the music would transform her humdrum suburban life to an extraordinarily beautiful one.

She would remember her childhood in the tropical plains of Assam. They lived in a large house which was divided into two with a large courtyard in between.

The front of the house had wide cement steps leading up to the dining room, sitting room and the bedrooms. There were many bedrooms, Molly remembers some rooms were only opened when they had guests, like their grandparents or their aunts.

The back of the house was a long building housing a few storage rooms and a large wood burning kitchen. One of storage rooms became a hen house while the other one was used as intended, for supplies.

The washroom was a little house between the two buildings, it had a hand pump, called a tube well then and a large cement bath for storing water. The maid would keep the cement bath full of water so that anyone wanting to have a bath could then dip a pail in the water and then pour it over themselves.

The toilets were to one side, the typical outhouse, under a large breadfruit tree so that if you went to toilet after sunset you could hear the leaves crunching underfoot but not much else by the light of the hurricane lamp. There was a well that grown-ups could draw water from using a pulley system, sadly children were not allowed to use it.

Molly was in year four then and she and her brother both attended the same government school nearby. Molly's dad used to drop them before work while Molly's mum picked them up in the afternoon.

It was at this time that Molly's mum had a crazy friend who knitted all day so she too started knitting all day; she made shawls and covers and blankets like they were going out of fashion. For one of her shawls, she needed a special frame, this was a huge structure of wood full of rows of nails and the shawl was made by winding the wool over and around the nails in a certain way.

Once they were firmly wound, they had to be trimmed with sharp scissors, and the whole process was laborious.

Molly's brother Sam had calmed down a lot so that having all those nails sticking out and the use of sharp scissors was not an issue. Truth be told, Sam spent very little time indoors, he was out playing football with his friends, trying to climb the large coconut tree in front, trying to ride a bicycle four sizes too big for him and just generally exploring. He was a great favourite in the neighbourhood in spite of his mischievous ways and would be asked to share lunch/dinner with any family if he was around. By the time he came in late evening, he had just enough energy to wash and change into his night suit before crashing.

Molly remembers Sam had once forgotten to wash his feet so Molly's mum asked her to clean his feet. Sam was already fast asleep so Molly got a large towel, dipped it in warm water and then cleaned her brother's feet. Sam knew nothing; he slept right through it as one does in childhood. Molly was the exact opposite of her brother's dynamic character in her childhood; she was a quiet, soft spoken, contemplative type of person.

When it started raining, young girls her age would run out and get wet in the rain. Not for Molly, she would pull up a chair next to one of the large windows and just sit and watch the rain for hours. No one had asked her, what are you watching? What is there to watch? It's just rain, right? It's a good thing no one asked because Molly would not be able to tell them why she loved watching the rain. It's Not Just Rain, never.

After coming to England, she had gotten used to the quiet drizzle that is so characteristic of this country and its people. Rain in India is like the country and the people, it is noisy and dramatic with lightning and rolling thunder and the sweet vapour rising from the warm soil afterwards.

Molly thinks about all the countries suffering with drought and feels if only we could build a huge blower and blow all the rain clouds from here to the dry regions of the world, we would be able to stop hunger, famine, war and so many other problems that arise from the lack of rain.

Chapter 27

Remember Kali, the super adventurous mummy hen who was laying and hatching eggs in the back of Molly's dad's ambassador? Well, Kali is now quite matronly and she has a lovely brood of babies. Molly remembers one pure white cock with a deep red beard, he was so good looking. Kali was still adventurous, she would lay eggs anywhere, literally. Once the maid was folding the mosquito net and found two eggs carefully ensconced in the folds. Kali continued to have children for the next few years before retiring.

Their house in Assam was more of a country house, there were quite a few papaya trees, a large breadfruit tree and a well for drawing ground water. The house was set on a large plot with lots of flowering trees in the front and fruit trees at the back. You could tell that no one was fighting over each centimetre of land when they built this house. It was large, comfy and totally unpretentious.

Molly remembers the large wooden dining table that they all sat at for meals, for parties, for playing word games, for everything. It was the centre of the household. Molly being the quiet one spent more time there than her brother who was always out exploring the neighbourhood.

If that table could speak, it would tell you of rushed breakfasts, of noisy birthday parties, of Mum's knitting group, weekend word making sessions, card playing competitions and much more.

Molly remembers this was a mofussil town and none of the cinema halls had English films. Yay, this meant Molly and her brother were allowed to go to Bengali and Hindi films (carefully checked by grown-ups in advance), for the first time. It felt so grown up going to watch films like *Hum Kisise Kam Nahin* or *Joy Baba Taraknath* with parents and sometimes grandparents too.

The samosas and jalebis after the film were hot and sweet and just fantastic and Molly knew that this was the sole reason her brother was sitting in the same seat for more than two hours, at a time. The grown-ups had tea, of course, and the children would have Fanta or Limca. There was no alcohol about then, none at all. The people who drank alcohol in those days were either very rich or very poor. The middle class looked at it with a healthy disregard, which worked just fine. Molly remembers reading in newspapers about poor people drinking adulterated alcohol and going blind from the side effects. It was scary. Looking back, the only worry Molly had then was her homework for next day but all she wanted was to grow up, now she knows growing up's not a good idea, not at all.

Once, Molly's mum was cleaning a fish when she got a small fishbone stuck in her hand. By the end of next week, the whole hand was swollen and septic, Molly's mum had to go to hospital for a week while they did dressings and gave her injections. Molly remembers thinking how brave her mum must be to go and take the injections all by herself, because the hospital outpatient appointments were during the day when her dad was at work.

Molly's grandparents would come and stay with them sometimes but it was difficult because they had responsibilities and commitments back in Kolkata which could only be done remotely for so long.

Molly's granddads were great friends, one a retired company executive, the other a retired police detective, Narcotics branch.

They would go to the village market two days a week—Tuesdays and Saturdays; Molly's mum was glad she did not have to do the food shopping anymore. Once the shopping was home, it was in Mum's court and she would plan the menu and then direct the servants.

Once they were back, Molly was called in with an exercise book and a pencil. Her granddads would give her the list of what they bought and how much it cost. Molly would draw up the list and add up the prices to give the total cost of the shopping. This was meant to be training for the future, when Molly will have her own household and will have to keep track of spending. Molly is not sure whether she learnt anything about finance or accounting from those sessions but it was fun sitting with her granddads, listening to them discussing what the items were, how the shopkeeper was trying to rip them off with high prices, how they got a real bargain in the end. She remembers it like it was yesterday.

The days they did not go shopping, Molly was called in again but this time with two newspapers, one English one Bengali.

She had to go through the main headlines in both newspapers, her granddads would choose which headlines they found interesting and Molly was asked to read the article. The English paper was *The Statesman,* of course and to this day, some names have stuck in her brain—the foreign correspondents Warren Unna from Washington, Paul Chutkow from Paris, to name a few.

She also remembers the politics very clearly because she was reading the newspapers aloud.

Even now, if someone mentions Chikmagalur, she knows this was where Mrs Gandhi declared an emergency, little things like that have stuck. Molly is not sure if children now get to spend much quality time with grandparents. She can see the grandparents making a huge effort when the grandchildren are babies. They move their jobs about and some even sell up and relocate so they can babysit, the parents are interested too as childcare costs an arm and a leg in this country and its win-win, probably. But as soon as the children reach an age where they can interact with the grandparents, listen to their stories, go for walks, play cards and the like, the children and the parents have unknowingly and very likely involuntarily drifted away from the grandparents.

Molly, like other kids in her generation, spent a lot of time with her grandparents and she would not change it for the world. It was a beautiful time and people who have not grown up with their grandparents have missed out on a beautiful part of their childhood.

Chapter 28

Letter to my son:

Sometimes when the body is in great distress, the mind is at its most productive.

You would expect that when the body was in distress, the mind would be numbed but no, the greater the body's distress the sharper the clarity of the mind. It's as if the body is trying to distract itself from the pain. Molly remembers being very ill with a fever and a cough a few years back. The cough started as soon she tried to lie down, and this went on for days that was when she perfected the art of sleeping while sat up, there was no other way.

She sat up in bed with three pillows scrunched behind her and started a letter to her little prince.

How are you, my prince? I know you have joined uni recently and I am dying to know how you are doing, whether classes have started already, how many friends you made and a million other really important things. I last saw you more than a year ago and every day I have missed you, missed you so much that I felt my heart breaking into a thousand pieces. How I longed to hold you, laugh with you about silly Indian soaps, when you tried all your accents on me, we used to have such fun.

I still wonder what happened and whether you miss me at all. I heard that you appeared for Oxbridge but did not get through. Never mind, you will teach at Oxbridge instead.

Have any of your school friends gone to the same uni? I remember I had one friend from school who went to uni with me and we were very close initially, probably because we did not know many people then. There was never any ill feelings or harsh words but we drifted slowly apart as we made our own friends.

But that's me, and I want to know about you. How's the food in uni? How are the student halls? Are they okay or really cool? I would love to know. I get up in the middle of the night and my face is wet and my pillow soaked through.

No marks for guessing why, I start looking for pictures of you on Facebook, looking up friends I have not met in a century, I go through their posts and try to scan each group photo to find you.

I am not always disappointed, sometimes I find one or two group pictures with you at one side so that I can crop the picture and keep it on my phone. You are such a handsome young man now, I feel proud but I miss the baby-you more, you were the very definition of chubby. I have not seen a rounder, sweeter, happier baby in my life.

You were not so happy initially though, you kept crying and crying for hours and days and weeks when you were about five weeks old, until one Tuesday at 2 am, we took you to hospital, concerned that there is something seriously wrong with you.

The on-call paediatric doctor took barely five minutes and came back to us with her diagnosis, this child is hungry. We stared at her in utter disbelief, she must be joking? At two in the morning on a busy shift? Seeing we were both medics, she understood that we were struggling to grasp what she had just said. "Are you sure? He has been crying for weeks now."

She smiled and said, "Okay, I see it's difficult for both of you to accept but I will prove it, I have just asked one of the girls to get me a bottle of milk from the ward."

The bottle of milk arrived, a medium sized bottle meant for older babies but you polished it off in three seconds flat and stopped crying too. I was trying to keep you off formula and in doing so, I had kept you hungry. I felt terribly guilty for doing this, though I was happy there was nothing seriously wrong.

So I came back from the hospital with two readymade bottles of milk kindly given by the registrar as all shops would be closed then.

We never looked back after that and you were the chubbiest and happiest baby in England. You loved milk and I remember Daddy saying that after you started, Cow and Gate have opened new factories and were taking on new staff, Daddy had a great sense of humour.

I remember you loved desserts and I used to buy the little jars of apple pie, strawberry cheesecake, raspberry trifle and the list went on. You would finish them off in a week or so. You have my sweet tooth alright. You know, sonny, I have very busy afternoons at work every day. I would be trying to describe a complicated management plan or discuss a complex report with a worried patient and I would be really deep in my work but somehow, I never miss the chimes of the ice cream van. They are silly and childish and repetitive and that's why I love those chimes.

They lift me straight out of the drudgery of work and transport me across decades in a fraction of a second to those happy times during school holidays when we knew the ice-cream van was coming and we planned what ice-cream we were having but we always forgot where the door keys were or where I had kept the loose change.

It was a lot of running around and laughing and panicking that the van would leave, but we somehow found the loose change and the door keys and always made it to the ice-cream van. Mission accomplished, we would be walking back to the house with our own ice-creams held high, laughing and talking.

When you grew up, life became so serious, I had to grow up too, sadly. I remember asking you to look after me when I am old, and you laughed and said, *Mummy, I will get a child-minder for you.* It was funny how you said that. Another time you wanted to watch one of those complicated films and because I did not understand what was going on, I fell asleep. To my utter embarrassment, I woke up to the sound of my snoring and saw you holding up a book trying to stop the light hitting my eyes. Awww, my baba.

I remember running around with you in the garden when you were nearly three. You were not speaking at all and at the last meeting, the health visitor had suggested that you be referred for speech therapy. I had accepted and was waiting for the appointment when this happened.

While running, I slipped and twisted my ankle so badly, I could not move. I called you and said go and call someone; Mummy needs help. You ran to the kitchen doors and kept hitting them with your little hands and you were trying to say help. I heard you saying help and knew we would not need speech therapy.

Why can I not see you? Why? It hurts so much, so much that I think I must have been a mass murderer or worse (not sure what is worse) in my last life to have had this punishment for my sins.

I will always love you, till the end of my days, my prince. Take good care and have a great time, god bless.

Chapter 29

A day off in the middle of the week.

Yippee. Sounds great. Even though Molly is totally skint and should be working every hour, God sends to pay her bills, she did not feel one bit guilty about not working one weekday.

From getting up late to taking her doggie for a long walk and then cooking dinner, it was all going swimmingly well.

She decided it should be fruit for dessert. They had brought some big oranges, so she cut them into mini chunks and put them in the fridge ready for after dinner. This worked really well especially if you have had a large greasy meal, it helped cut through the oil, freshened your mouth and felt so much better than eating sweet dessert or ice-cream.

She remembers the first time she ate sliced oranges for dessert was in a little Chinese restaurant just a few doors down from her old house. She always wanted to go out for dinner but Molloy was always coming up with good reasons for not going out. The reasons ranged from work to weather, his stomach issues to finances, and Molly had nearly given up when this little Chinese place across the road advertised a dinner deal. Maybe Molloy was also tired of trying to find excuses so he came along and it was really nice to just walk down from the house to the restaurant. Molly remembers they started with sake, Japanese wine. The sake was in a tiny glass that sat in a bath of steaming water. They had never drunk warm wine before and Molly was intrigued, this was different indeed. Molloy was not impressed, why warm the wine? Whoever drank this anyway?

Molly laughed then but made a mental note to look into this. She later read that Japan was a very cold country so warm wine was welcome when it was all frozen white outside. In contrast, some really warm places put salt into their beer as they sweated a lot trying to replace the salts lost by sweating, so the local beer reflected the area of the world it came from. The three courses were of good standard and they really enjoyed the food. The dessert was a bowl of cool sliced oranges and it was beautiful. The acidity cut through the oil and it was just the right level of sweet. Molly remembers they walked back to the house a happy couple talking about how well the oranges matched the menu.

Did they guess that five years later they would be divorced and Molly would be alone trying to build her own life? Probably not.

Happiness is like dewdrops on blades of grass. It is beautiful but does not last long. The only things that last long are chronic diseases like arthritis and old wooden furniture, everything else seems to disappear under the harsh gaze of reality.

Molly chopped the oranges, taking care to remove all the seeds to make sure they were just the right size, not too small or too big before putting them in a box to cool for dessert.

She drives past the little Chinese place sometimes, wondering if they still do dinner deals, with sake for appetiser and chilled oranges for dessert.

Chapter 30

Any discussion of Molly's life would be incomplete without a discussion of death.

Can you describe day without night? How would you describe one without reference to the other? Without death, life becomes a fake, two-dimensional construct. Once you discuss both life and death, you see them both clearly, both parts make perfect sense then.

Molly has thought about ending her life on several occasions. She knows from speaking to patients that this is not uncommon, or rather it's commoner than we like to think it is.

However, it is a cowardly act and though Molly has been called many names in the course of her life, even her most malicious critic would not call her a coward. Most definitely not.

"When I die," she has told her close friends and family, "don't make a fuss, just cremate my body, have a small celebration of my life, not a long faced memorial service with speeches and give any money left to a kids' charity." This has been her standard request over the last few years. Her friends listen half seriously and Molly is not quite sure that they will remember when the time comes.

Chapter 31

Molly was driving to work when her car started pulling to the left, it was strange, the steering wheel was really heavy and try as she might, she could not keep the car straight on the road.

She pulled into a layby (phew, that was close) and rang the AA. It seemed nearly everyone else in the country was also broken down by the roadside but they were broken down by the motorway or had kids with them, etc., so Molly was close to the bottom of their list. Being fully aware of this even before she rang them, Molly tried to settle down for the long wait. Radio was out as it might affect the battery life, it was warm so thank God she did not need any blankets.

There were a few tins of soup in the boot, sort of stand-by lunch but she was not hungry or thirsty but she really needed the loo. This was a country lane leading to the dual carriageway so there weren't any big stops like you have on the motorway with coffee and sandwiches and loos and bingo machines.

She was trying her best to distract herself when she saw a big lorry drive sharply into the layby, narrowly missing the back of Molly's car.

"Hey there mister, have you left your glasses at home? You need them."

"My glasses? Oh I see."

"Oh no you don't see, you don't see at all, you nearly hit the back of my car, I am already down with a burst tyre and you…"

"Oh is that the problem? Let me help you, do you have a spare?"

"No thank you very much. I am waiting for the AA."

"The AA? How long did they say the wait will be? That too on a day like this. Let me help you and you can be on your way in ten minutes."

"Really? You can sort this in ten minutes? Are you kidding me?"

"No, I am not. I would like to help if you would let me." "Hmm, you want to help me?"

"Yes, is that so strange?"

"Okay, ten minutes and not a second more then." "Sure, let me see now."

And to Molly's utter dismay, he seemed to know what he was doing and her car was back on the road in ten minutes as promised. Molly was embarrassed at how she had misbehaved with the gentleman; James Fleming was his name.

He had said—my friends call me Jimmy by the way—and lifted his T-shirt to show the large tattoo on his waist, Jimmy, written in cursive writing style.

"I am really sorry for speaking like I did and thank you for helping me out."

"Maybe you need a coffee after all this stress; just saying."

"Coffee? That's the last thing I need, I am dying for the loo and—"

"Oh, there's one just around the corner, get in your car and follow me."

This seemed to be a sound suggestion and for once, Molly just got into her car without arguing and followed the truck to the nearest forecourt—one of those places where you can fill your car, go to the loo, buy coffee and crisps, some even have freshly baked pies and all but this one was a no—frills place most definitely.

The cakes and sandwiches were at least a decade old but never mind it had a working loo.

Going to the loo, washing her face and having a drink of water from her car boot, Molly felt more like a human being and less like a water tank about to burst.

Mr Fleming was talking casually to the guy at the counter, they seemed to know each other. They both turned when Molly came in.

"Thank you so much for letting me use your toilet." "You are welcome, ma'am."

Molly turned to her saviour, "I really cannot thank you enough."

"No problem at all, sure you don't want a coffee?"

"I have patients waiting so I really cannot waste any more time."

"Well, I need to be getting along too, get the wheel checked by a mechanic as soon as you can, think there's one right next to your clinic."

"I will, thanks again, Mr Fleming."

"Jimmy to you, cheers, all the best."

They both drove off from there and soon enough, Molly was trying to catch up on a waiting room full of patients, she totally forgot about her car. The weekend came and went, hours of studying for her appraisal, all the cooking washing ironing for the week and Molly felt exhausted on Monday. She should have booked in advance with the garage next to her surgery because she knew they were always booked up for weeks. As she waited for them to pick up, she knew they would be fully booked for the whole week at least.

Just my luck, thought Molly. She was in for a surprise.

"Dr Mitter, your car's booked for a wheel check today at 2 pm."

"Oh, who booked my car?"

"Who booked it? A gentleman rang on Friday, said he was booking your car, he gave us the car details, so we knew it was your car all right."

"Hoh okay, I will leave the keys at reception."

"Thanks Doctor."

Ha, what does he think of himself? Who gave him the right to book my car? He is probably trying to help, maybe. Never mind, one less thing to do and to hell with everything else. Molly dived into the pile of papers on her desk.

Chapter 32

It was especially humid that night—muggy, as per Molly's second language Mancunian.

Lying awake in bed in between innumerable glasses of water and the resultant trips to the loo, Molly thought of this guy who had helped her with her car and even booked it for a wheel check. Was he just being charitable or was there something else going on?

Molly felt lonely coming to an empty house after work every evening, there was no one to talk to, no one to tell how the day had gone, no one to plan things with.

But look at the flipside, Molly told herself, no one to tell you what to do, ring you every two minutes each time you were out, make laughing stock out of you, the list was long. It was definitely better to be alone than trying to adjust to the wrong person. Some of her friends suggested a dating website but she knew these places from her single colleagues. Nearly everyone fibbed about everything. There was hardly any truth in their personal info. There was no point spending hard earned money to get hurt again, that much Molly knew.

So, when she saw Mr call-me-jimmy Fleming filling up his truck at the same station, she was pleasantly surprised. They exchanged pleasantries and decided to go for that much-talked-about long-overdue cup of coffee. It was a Tuesday evening and she only worked Wednesday afternoon, so there was no mad rush to go back to an empty home.

Molly ordered a toasted ham and cheese sarnie with her coffee, this was her favourite and in Molly's books, ham and cheese and coffee were the perfect trio, they blended and complemented each other perfectly. What did James's order with his coffee? Probably a falafel sandwich, if Molly's memory served her right.

They sat in the coffee shop talking and drinking coffee that wet Tuesday evening until it was time to go home. Molly felt comfortable and relaxed and when James suggested they meet next Tuesday at the same place, she agreed.

Molly felt they were becoming good friends in the last few weeks, she liked to sit and talk to him about the week, about her work her patients her colleagues and about everything really. James listened patiently, asked questions about the medical side of things and was generally approving of Molly except when it came to the car.

"You don't look after your car, doctor."

"What do you mean? It's taxed, mooted and all the rest."

"That's just the legal bit, that's not looking after your car."

"Oh ok, what is looking after the car then? Washing it daily? Polishing it weekly? Monthly valet? Tell me, Mr Fleming."

"Well, when was the last time you washed the car?"

"I don't remember, I must've washed it sometime."

"You haven't washed the car in the last few weeks that we have been meeting for coffee."

"I see your point, but the car belongs to me and I decide when it needs washing or polishing."

"I suppose you could say that again, doc."

"Thank you, Mr Fleming."

Molly liked to listen to him talk about his week at work, his weekend with his parents in Sheffield and about his two nieces in Glasgow. James was close to his family and spent all his holidays with them.

Molly had been meeting James at the same coffee place for a couple of years now. If Molly could not make it on Tuesday, they would meet on another weekday suitable to both. They never met over the weekend, they were happy sitting and talking over coffee and sandwiches once a week. Molly often wondered where this was going, then she thought, *Why does it have to go anywhere because I am happy with where it is now and James seems happy too, so why not park it here for now.*

They were good friends and Molly did not want to risk their friendship over some stupid romantic notion. She liked him too much to risk losing his friendship.

Molly decided not to tell her friends because she felt they would not understand. Not that she understood it either.

Chapter 33

Molly was in Kolkata visiting her parents and they were travelling to her uncle's house at the other end of the city. Molly wanted to get chocolates for her nephew and her niece and was just walking down to the store while her parents were locking up, when she suddenly felt she had gone back three decades and was going to meet her ex, her first love. She felt young, happy and light on her feet. She could see the tall slender dark young man coming down to meet her. He was at least a foot taller than her, six years older, from a totally different background but all of that was not important, these silly facts faded into a mist when they met.

There was so much love so much hope so much happiness it was magical. When did it all start to go downhill? When did they stop loving each other? It must be like cancer, a few erratic cells tucked away in a corner of the body no symptoms until it decides to declare itself very humbly, sometimes with a stomach upset, a cough or a rash.

The body/person thinks, *Ahh this will clear soon, I have had this a million times and it's cleared, until he/she finds out that although this looks similar, it's different to what's happened before and it's here to stay.*

So maybe Molly and Molloy had a fight and both of them thought, *Oh, it's fine, we have done this and gone back to our usual selves a million times—until the time when the fights, disagreements and rows become more and more common and the cancer of Unlove raises its ugly head.*

So just as a stomach upset is not a stomach upset, it's bowel cancer, the disagreement is not just a row, it's divorce and like cancer, it's here to stay.

Molly's children had told her several times and in no uncertain terms that the divorce was her fault. At times, even her mother said that, and for what? Just to win an argument.

Seeing her nephew and niece today brought back fond memories of her children when they were young and soft and cuddly like toys. When their parents complained, Molly tried to tell them that they will be grown up and gone soon, "They are not little for long, you know," but it's impossible for busy young mums to understand this, Molly did not know it then either.

"Mummy, I can't see you."

"Here I am, my baba."

"But I cannot see you, I cannot see you."

"Why can't you see me? Why can't you see me?"

"It's too dark, it's too dark."

"Let me see, ah you have covered your face with the duvet."

"Why can't I see through the duvet, Mummy?"

"Because it's not transparent."

"What's that?"

"Let me get your glass of milk, baba."

"Please can I have a biscuit, Mummy?"

Molly loved her children and missed them no less than any mother but she did not want anyone to see her pain, she did not want to share what she considered her personal tragedy.

But of course, in all tiny expat communities like the Indian community in her hometown, her personal tragedy was the subject of gossip.

For the bored housewives with rich husbands who went away on tours and children in university, the fact that she appeared normal, spoke and laughed and reacted as the next person meant she did not miss her children. To them she had just walked out on her children, while Molly was working all possible hours and taking out loan after loan from the banks to pay for lawyers to fight for her children, they were out partying and shopping.

When Molly ran out of money and the banks refused to loan her any more, she came home and sold her wedding jewellery to raise the sums. It was not right but there was no other way as her dad had retired few years back and her mum had never worked. Molly felt sad about selling her jewellery but did not quite know what else to do for money.

Though Molly had very rich friends both at home and in England, they all had excellent reasons as to why they could not loan the money to Molly. The reasons were varied but it all came down to—I am so sorry that I cannot help you; is there anything else that you need help with, dear; don't worry, I understand this is a difficult time for you. There will never be a right time to lend money to your dear friend, and that's why you are rich, because you don't hand out money, even though you claim to be my closest friend and keep telling me how much you worry about me every day.

Amazing world.

When Molly was in school, money was the root of all evil. In life, nothing happens without it. Literally nothing. So why we were not told how important money is, how to handle, when to spend, how to save etc. Never taught never discussed and this was one of the most important aspects of adult life.

One could say the same about sex but that was then. Molly knows there is sex education in all schools nowadays. Good for the students. The only bit of sex education Molly got was from her biology book in class twelve. She had few friends in school and was a quiet bookish type, so there was not much chance of learning from anywhere else. Not just bookish, maybe a little snooty, Molly looked down upon the popular romantic series of her time and did not read a single one.

So, her birds and bees came from the fat biology book with black and white diagrams of clearly labelled body parts and their functions, as expected from a biology text book. So the students who did not study biology would have to rely on hearsay and stories to find out about sex. There were no search engines in those days and parents were not sure what to tell the children, having had no sex education themselves.

But at least we have made moves in that direction by including sex education in the curriculum, whereas where money is concerned, students are still being dangerously short-changed.

Chapter 34

Back at work after a fortnight off and no time for jetlag, Molly always went to work the day after she landed and promised to get sleep over the weekend.

It was not easy especially because her tiredness had worsened since Covid but she knew there was no other way to do this she would have to pace herself and take short breaks of ten or fifteen minutes in-between patients. Her last but one patient was a little girl with congenital adrenal hyperplasia and Mum was coming in to discuss medication. The little notes next to the patient's name were not always right as the patient or parent did not like telling reception staff what they were coming for, so when the note said medication review, it could have been anything under the sun.

To Molly's surprise, it was exactly that, Mum was worried she was not getting the meds delivered regularly and she wanted to discuss the doses of steroids the little girl was on. The patient, the little girl in this case suffered with a condition where her body was deficient of an enzyme, this led to a deficiency of steroids produced by the body and also led to masculinising features like the growth of the clitoris.

This little girl was on set doses of steroids three times daily with higher doses for sick days. The letter also suggested operation to reduce the size of the clitoris. Molly looked at Mum, earnestly talking about the chemist and wondered whether Mum was using the chemist as a distraction.

What is it like to have a baby girl with male-ish genitalia? Not easy at all. She could imagine the gossip that must be going on in the family and marvelled at the strength of the mother. She was talking and reacting normally and if Molly had not read the notes, she would never be able to guess what an ordeal life had dealt her.

Mum was now asking Molly whether all the steroids she was giving her little girl would have any side effects. Molly explained that we are giving her the steroids to replace the steroids that we all make naturally in our bodies, so it will do no harm.

Molly discussed the problems with the chemist delivering late as naturally as possible and offered Mum a change of chemist, Mum agreed to think about it and get back.

It was always the same, patients and parents with serious conditions always spoke and behaved very normally, as if everything was fine whereas those with earache, sore throat and acne always gave her the impression that they were on their death bed. This innate love of drama is omnipresent, sadly.

Maybe it was not drama, maybe it's all about perception. We expect seriously ill patients to be serious about their illness and not-so-seriously ill patients to be not-so-serious about their illness but the reverse is true. Patients with brain tumours and lung cancers smile and speak so normally that Molly has to glance back at the screen to make sure this is the right patient. Yes, this is the patient with the highly malignant glioma but he was talking about the weather.

Molly admired their courage in the face of death their normality when faced with severe pain/discomfort. It was quite unimaginable what the patients and their families went through, even the best healthcare in the world can only go so far.

She was walking back to her car after work on a Wednesday. It was about 8 pm; the temperature a chilling 2 degrees and a strange lull in the air. The energy of Monday/Tuesday evening or the excitement of Thursday/Friday evening were both absent. There was instead a feeling of being in a vacuum. Molly noticed a small flashing light on her right, after a few minutes she realised it was the street light reflecting off her steel flask. The flask was still half full, Molly had not drunk much coffee today.

Her stomach felt off for some reason and she had stayed off coffee, thinking it will make her feel worse. In fact, earlier today she had wondered whether she should go home but decided to stay and finish her clinic. It was always like this Molly could never gather enough strength/or enough weakness to ever decide: I am not well, I need to go home.

She would start arguing with herself and after about half an hour of arguing with herself she would decide it was much easier to stay than to convince herself to leave. She had worked through toothache/earache/twisted ankle and the like. On balance, Molly was sure nearly every doctor had done or does what she was doing today. It was part of the job, well, nearly.

Chapter 35

It was a hot summer night in India and Molly was staying over at her nana's place with her aunts and cousins.

In her nana's bedroom, with the polished red floors and the beautifully carved mahogany bed, Molly was sleeping with her aunt and her mum. As she was about to fall asleep, one of her mum's uncles came and laid down on the far side of the bed. Molly still remembers this but she was only thirteen and she was sleeping between her aunt and her mum. Compared to present day, her thirteen-year-old brain was probably the same as a five-year-old in the present, but that's by the by.

Molly woke up at night, it was pitch dark, but she could feel her mum's uncle's hand between her legs, trying to get inside her undies. She was so scared she did not know what to do and tried to lie very still. The hand kept groping between her legs and found a way inside. Molly was now very uneasy, she wanted to scream, she wanted to run but kept lying as still as possible.

The hand started moving up and down between her legs and Molly wanted to sneeze. She woke up and sat up in bed, sneezing and crying and waking her mum and aunt from their sleep.

She remembers they were very surprised and kept asking why Molly woke them up. Molly was crying so hard she was not making any sense. She went to the toilet, washed her face and her legs and stood in the wide balcony, crying aloud and waiting for the sun to come up.

Molly does not remember exactly what happened later except that her mum's uncle left abruptly before breakfast. Nobody talked about what happened or did anything or asked Molly. It was as if nothing had happened.

Molly started keeping a safe distance from Mum's uncle and avoided meeting him/talking to him. Even when she was grown up and married, she could not bear to be in the same room with him, even if it was a family wedding.

In fact, Molly's mum tried to talk her out of it. "You are overreacting."

"How I react is my business, why did you not look after me, ma?"

"It was an accident."

"Wish Baba was there, he would have given Uncle a solid thrashing."

"Don't talk like that, he is a senior in the family."

"Senior? He is worse than an animal, ma, how can you put up with this?"

"Put up with what?"

"You are right, ma, it's not you, it's me, I am not putting up with this, I am not going to this stupid wedding."

"Have it your way, you never listen to me, don't know why I even try."

And so it went for many a family wedding until Molly moved abroad after marriage and thank goodness there was little or no chance of meeting Mr Groper.

Molly learnt later that he passed but even to this day, she struggles to forgive or forget what happened that hot summer night when she was barely thirteen and had trusted her mum and her aunt to look after her. She used to be very careful with her daughter, trying to warn her of the dangers as soon as she was old enough—don't trust anyone, sweetie, you never know how people are and how they might change.

Molly's little girl listened quietly, wide-eyed, trying to understand why her happy-go-lucky mum was so tense when she explained these things.

Chapter 36

Lightly o lightly we bear her along
she sways like a flower in the wind of our song she skims like
a star on the foam of a stream she floats like a laugh from the
lips of a dream gaily o gaily we glide and we sing
we bear her along like a pearl on a string

~Song of palanquin bearers (Sarojini Naidu)

Even before Molly wanted to be a journalist, she wanted to be a poet. She loved poetry and even though she forgot everything else, she did not forget the poetry she had read. This was not only weird but exhilarating and when she was in the right mood, the poetry came bubbling out of her. People around her were initially surprised then impressed to find she could quote nonstop from memory—something she had read decades ago. When it rained, she would usually tell her children:

I hear leaves drinking rain I hear rich leaves on top giving the poor beneath drop after drop 'tis a sweet noise to hear these green leaves drinking near Mr Auto Fleming, as she tended to call him sometimes, was not averse to poetry and Molly could just be herself and recite long pieces of poetry like, "How they brought the good news…" and he would listen, quietly enjoying the piece. This was important for Molly as she could relax and be herself and not have to worry about what he might be thinking.

Their casual coffee-on-the-go meetings have become a regular thing now and one time, when Molly was down with a bad chest, she realised she looked forward to them and maybe even missed Mr Fleming.

Oh no no no. Not again, Molly told herself. I am not going down this slippery slope called love. Most definitely not. Have I not had enough hurt humiliation and insult for a lifetime? Enough and some more, to be honest.

The funny thing was that Mr Fleming hardly said anything outside of normal. They chatted about everything under the sun except themselves. Molly thought many times about asking him to come home but then, they were not together, were they, so maybe asking him to come home was not the right thing to do.

Things continued ticking over till one fine Sunday morning, Molly was coming down the stairs and she missed the bottom step, fell and broke her ankle. Her neighbours called the ambulance, she was taken straight to theatre and came home with her left foot in plaster walking on crutches. For the first week, Molly just woke up, took her painkillers and went back to sleep.

After the first week, she was a bit more awake but she did not feel strong enough to do anything except clean her teeth and boil the kettle for tea. Taking a shower was a challenge as Molly's shower was inside her bath and climbing in the bath with the plastered leg was too tricky. So she had to make do with towelling her body with a hot wet towel and washing her hair in the basin. It was messy but it was all she could manage. Mr Fleming rang on his usual day.

"Where are you, doc, I am here at the coffee shop."

"Oh, I am at home."

"Sorry to disturb you, did not realise you were on leave."

"Wait wait, don't be sorry, I am not on leave, I meant I am on leave, its sick leave."

"Are you all right? Sick leave? What happened?"

"I broke my ankle and I have to rest for the next 12 weeks."

"How in heavens name did you do that?"

"I fell down the stairs, last Sunday."

"Is it okay to come and see you? I am worried."

"Ah, I guess it is."

"Thanks, text me your address and let me know if you need anything from the shops."

That was how Molly's secret plan of I-will-not-call-him-to-the-house-because-we-are-not-together failed in grand exuberant style.

Visit? Ha ha, Mr Fleming became a regular and by the end of the first week had his own set of keys to the front door as Molly's ankle did not let her move as much or as fast. He came in, checked the fridge and the cupboards, went out and was back in a couple of hours with groceries.

He had brought a little wooden seat for Molly so she could sit in the bath and take a shower while sitting in the bath, her plastered leg wrapped in a plastic sheet.

When he left late that evening, Molly had had a shower after four days, had a hot soup and toast dinner and felt a million times better than she did the day before.

"I will come and see you tomorrow if I can, text me if you need anything, doc."

"Goodnight Mr Fleming."

When she heard the door close behind him, Molly had a wide smile on her face. It felt so good to have him around. He did not do any of the things Molly disliked. How did he know what she disliked?

All Molly knew was, yes, this was probably the slippery slope but boy it felt fantastic.

Twelve weeks is a long time for someone not used to stopping for a second, Molly felt restless initially but Mr Fleming's visits somehow calmed her, she was eating and sleeping better. *They will have to get a locum, thank god no one else was on leave now, it gets really tight if two doctors are off at the same time.*

The day she was finally free of the plaster cast, Molly decided to celebrate by going out, of course. She had stayed at home for 12 weeks except for hospital appointments. This was a record for her, she had never stayed at home for such a long time. Even when her kids were born, she worked till a week before the delivery date and started going out with them after four weeks, that too because Molly's mum was here for the delivery and would not let her go out with the baby before four weeks.

Molly liked comfy places where people go for the food, not the decor or the waiters so she chose one that she liked a lot. A no-nonsense Chinese place run by a family from Canton.

Her leg felt a bit funny after being in plaster for so many days so Molly decided to wear slacks and a silk top, in keeping with the Chinese theme. Her hair had grown, so she just brushed it back and tied it in a ponytail. Before leaving the house, Molly just glanced in the mirror in the hallway and she was surprised to see how beautiful she looked, as if lit up from inside. I am a Chinese lantern, she thought smiling as she climbed into her car. As Molly walked across the restaurant, she could see Mr Fleming waiting. He had brought her flowers, lilies, in fact.

"Here you go, doc, got you these."

"Oh thank you, I love lilies."

"You scrubbed up all right too."

"Ahh, yes. Shall we order? I am starving."

Molly was not very good with compliments; she became embarrassed and forgot to say thank you. Silly woman, when will you ever learn!

Chapter 37

It was that time of year, to other people it was a time of happiness and good cheer but for Molly, and for a lot of her patients, this was a dreaded time of year.

This was the time when Molly remembered how she decorated the tree and the house, how she went shopping with her daughter for company but also because her daughter remembered the ages of all their friends' kids, how she baked for Christmas and other painful details crowded into her mind. She had spent every Christmas after divorce without her children, even though she has made endless pleas to the courts and the social workers that she wanted to see her children for Christmas. Somehow it had always been impossible to travel the few miles between their houses to see their mum for Christmas. So each Christmas, Molly just cried and wished she could see her children.

This year, she was not only lonely but she was poor as well. She had started home improvements but underestimated the cost of living and now she was heavily in debt. She owed her bank 20K which she was paying off monthly and she owed two of her friends 5K each.

This had been a really tough time for her and she had promised not to buy any presents for anyone. She dug out some Christmas cards lying in a drawer from last year and sent them off, second-class of course.

The trouble was when friends invited her, she had to take a gift. The best option was to go back to baking, cakes made the perfect present especially at this time of year and did not break the bank.

She had been worried about her gas and electric, this had been in the news and with rising interest rates, things were bound to get tighter very soon. The saddest part was that she loved Christmas and in her hometown in India, Christmas was a festival. All the streets were lighted and full of people partying till the small hours of the morning. Put that with her convent education, Molly loved everything about Christmas. The tree, the lights, the carols, the cakes, the roast dinner and buying presents for her children. Molly was lost in her own world when a sharp rap on the door brought her back. A delivery? She had not ordered anything.

She opened the door to find Mr Fleming outside.

"Can I come in, doc, it's freezing."

"Yes sure, it's very cold."

"Just wondered what you were doing for Christmas, doc."

"I thought you were with your family in Glasgow."

"They decided to go to Ibiza, doc, only told me last week."

"Oh I am sorry, you could have gone with them, couldn't you?"

"No doc, not my kind of holiday, they knew that."

"Even so, they should have, that's not fair, not at all."

"You still haven't told me what your plans are, doc."

"My plans? For Christmas?"

"Yes, that's my question, doc."

"Would you like a coffee? Your usual?"

"Do you have anything stronger at home?"

"There's some red wine."

"Let me get the glasses."

So they settled in front of the telly, with a bottle of red and some Doritos watching Notting Hill on telly, talking and laughing like the good friends that they were.

Looking back on that evening, Molly remembers every time a girlfriend asked friends for advice regarding someone, someone they were not sure that they loved or just liked, the advice was—get drunk and see what happens. Late that evening, after a dinner of pasta and salad with more red wine, Molly found herself kissing Mr Fleming on the sofa.

Strangely enough, he was not surprised at all. It was so natural, so soft and so easy as if they had been kissing for years. It felt so warm and so comfortable and Molly felt her whole body waking up in a way it had not done in years.

She wanted everything and she wanted it now. Even while she was undressing as fast as she could, she was thinking— this is all too quick.

But then she felt Mr Fleming's lips on hers and she could not think anymore.

"Morning doc." He had made her breakfast, toast with butter melting, coffee and eggs.

"Aww, you didn't have to do this."

"By the way, doc, you still haven't toldme your plans for Christmas."

"I have a brilliant plan now."

"Really? And what plan is that?"

"Let's just stay in bed, Mr Fleming."

"That's truly brilliant. I totally agree."

"Merry Christmas to you too."

Chapter 38

Molly took one last sip of cold black coffee before washing her blue steel flask at the sink in her office. She liked her flask but she hated the clinking noise it made when it touched anything metallic. She tried her best but both her workbag and her handbag had metal clasps so this made it impossible to avoid the clinking, especially when going home after a long day.

She had been looking for a flask that would not clink, because she did not wish to attract the attention of the patients and staff when she walked across the waiting area. Of course, they could see her that was not an issue but the sound was.

Struggling with her long coat, woollen scarf, handbag and heavy shoulder bag, she trundled towards the door, clinking with alternate step as her flask touched the metal clasps on her bag. *Two more steps and I am out.*

Have a great evening see you tomorrow doctor bye bye! And Molly was outside walking to her car. This was the best part of the day, all work done and looking forward to putting her feet up in front of the idiot box.

But she did not feel as good as usual. Too much coffee? Probably. She must've had about a litre of black coffee today, give or take a cup. *That can't be good for the body surely,* thought Molly, putting all her bags into the car.

As she started driving, she felt strange, like there was no air in the car. *Oh, nothing like plenty of fresh air after a long day cooped up indoors,* she thought, *pulling the windows down.*

In spite of the time of night, the traffic was quite heavy and people drove like they owned the road and were simply letting others use their road from the goodness of their heart. Once she reached home, Molly planned a shower and a short walk because that airless feeling was still there. It started raining so Molly had to put the windows up, worried the car seats will get wet. Strangely, she did not mind getting wet herself today that was so unlike her. In school, whenever her best friend wanted to walk in the rain, she had declined.

I must get home fast and have some Gaviscon, thought Molly, *this airless feeling is probably acid rising to my gullet.* She felt a weight on her chest and along with the airlessness felt she could not drive.

Really can't trouble anyone at this time, everyone's busy, thought Molly.

Both friends and colleagues were just finishing work or driving home. The problem was she could not drive but knew she needed to go to the hospital. Getting a taxi was the best option that did not waste anyone's time.

Good idea, thought Molly but she had to search for her phone in her huge bag and by the time she found her phone, she could not speak anymore.

She could hear a gruff voice at the other end, "Hello, taxi service, hello, why don't you speak up, hello, hello?"

Molly felt her hand getting weak, she could not hold her phone anymore and her vision was blurring too, like looking through a glazed window.